School Friends

Secrets, hopes and dreams...
School friends are for ever!

Collect the whole **School Friends** series:

Party at Silver Spires
Dancer at Silver Spires
Dreams at Silver Spires
Magic at Silver Spires
Success at Silver Spires
Mystery at Silver Spires

...all featuring the Emerald dorm girls

First Term at Silver Spires
Drama at Silver Spires
Rivalry at Silver Spires
Princess at Silver Spires
Secrets at Silver Spires
Star of Silver Spires

...all featuring the Amethyst dorm girls

Want to know more about **School Friends**?
Check out
www.silverspiresschool.co.uk

Magic
at
Silver
Spires

Ann Bryant

USBORNE

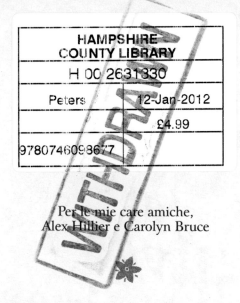
Per le mie care amiche,
Alex Hillier e Carolyn Bruce

First published in the UK in 2010 by Usborne Publishing Ltd.,
Usborne House, 83-85 Saffron Hill, London EC1N 8RT, England.
www.usborne.com

Cover illustration by Rui Ricardo for folioart.co.uk

The name Usborne and the devices ♀ ⊕ are Trade Marks of
Usborne Publishing Ltd.

A CIP catalogue record for this book is available from the British Library.

JFMAMJJASON /10 95198 ISBN 9780746098677
Printed in Reading, Berkshire, UK.

Chapter One

"**D**on't let me see it!" squealed Emily, covering her eyes dramatically.

"Oh sorry!" I said, quickly whipping the mask I'd almost finished painting away from my face, and hiding it behind my back.

Maybe this was another English thing I didn't know about. Perhaps there's a – what do you call it? – yes, a superstition that it's bad luck to wear a mask inside a building or something.

My best friend, Nicole, quickly reassured me. "Don't worry, Antonia," she said. "It's just that Emily likes surprises."

Across the room I could see Mr. Cary, the art teacher, shaking his head at Emily as though she was mad. But his eyes were twinkling.

"It'll be tons more fun when it comes to the Italian evening if we haven't seen each other's masks before," Emily added.

I agreed with Emily really, and that was why we six friends had been quite secretive when we'd been making and decorating our masks so far. But I just hadn't been able to resist showing mine off, which was stupid of me when I already know how exciting it is to see a mass of masks and have no idea whose faces are behind them. I can so clearly remember the thrill I felt when I set eyes on all the thousands of people dressed up in their masks at the *Carnevale* I went to with my family last February. The word "*carnevale*" is Italian for "carnival". And for Italian people like me, the one that takes place in Venice is the best one, not only in Italy, but in the whole world. Mamma and Papà and my two brothers and I had what I think you would call "the time of our lives" when we were there last year.

It feels so strange thinking about it now, here in the art room at Silver Spires Boarding School for Girls. Of course, I had absolutely no idea back then that I'd be coming to a school in England in September.

"Why don't we each just show our mask to our best friend so that they can check it's all right?" suggested sensible Sasha.

The rest of us thought that was a brilliant idea, except for Emily, who had nowhere near finished hers. But all the same, we went off in pairs with our masks into different corners of the art room.

"Hey, that's brilliant!" Nicole said when she saw mine properly.

Her eyes were all shiny and I could tell she really liked it, which was a big relief, as I was the one who came up with the idea of making masks in the first place. It all started when we came back to school after the spring half-term holiday, and Mrs. Pridham, our housemistress, announced that Forest Ash boarding house (which is where we live and is definitely the best boarding house, by the way) was to have an Italian evening during this half of term. I know she chose Italy because that's my home country, and I feel very – how do you say it? – yes, very touched.

"I'd like you to take a leading part in helping to organize the evening, Antonia," were Mrs. Pridham's exact words, spoken with her usual bright smile. "I need to pick your brains for ideas."

Then we'd both laughed, because I'd wrinkled

my nose in disgust at the thought of her picking my brains. I'd never heard that expression before. There's still so much English for me to learn, but at least now I can understand most things and I can usually manage to say whatever I want to say.

As it happened, I was bursting with ideas, because we love parties and festivals and carnivals in Italy, especially in my own family. *Mio papà* – sorry, my dad – owns a restaurant. He employs two chefs to do all the cooking there. Papà is a very well-known TV chef in Italy, so he doesn't have much time to cook at our lovely Ristorante Alessandro himself. He only does it on special occasions – usually when we're celebrating a birthday in our family or something like that, and then we decorate the whole restaurant and often dress up in fancy dress, and play Italian folk music, so the atmosphere is *brillante* – sorry, brilliant!

When I first came here last September at the beginning of Year Seven, if ever my mind slipped off into thoughts about my family and our lovely house in Milan, I would feel so homesick it was almost unbearable. But then Nicole and I became best *best* friends and that changed everything for me. I didn't feel alone any more. The other four girls in the dormitory – Izzy, Sasha, Emily and Bryony – had been very friendly and kind to me, but Nicole just hadn't seemed to like me at first. It all turned out to be a great big misunderstanding, thank goodness, and from the moment we got it all sorted out I felt like a new person. A person who could cope with all the differences between my old life in Italy at a day school and my new life in England at a boarding school.

When I came back after Christmas I realized I truly loved Silver Spires. Nicole taught me the expression *It's like a home from home*, and that's a good way of explaining how I feel now.

Nicole was touching the braid that I'd stuck on my mask around the holes for the eyes. Then her fingers moved to the part on one side that I'd painted gold. The paint was all dry because I'd done that bit first. "How did you get it to look like real gold, Antonia?" she asked me, frowning.

"By using many layers of paint," I told her.

"Lots of layers," she corrected me.

"Lots of layers," I repeated, feeling grateful, as I always do, that I've got someone to help me get better and better at English. I could hardly speak it at all last September, because Mamma and my grandparents on Mamma's side are all Italian, and Papà is half-Italian. His mum is English, so he speaks both languages, but we only ever speak Italian at home.

"Anyway, show me *your* mask, Nicole," I said, feeling excited as a sudden picture of the whole of Forest Ash wearing masks at the Italian evening flashed through my head.

"It's quite boring compared to yours," she said, quietly.

But it wasn't. For a start, her mask covered more of her face than mine did *and* it was in the shape of a cat's face, with whiskers and everything.

"It's totally fab!" I said. Then we both burst out laughing, because I'd only just learned that word and I was so proud of it I couldn't stop using it. "Fab, fab, fab!"

"That's the tenth time today!" Nicole said, giving me one of her teacher looks. "*Sei pazza!*" she added.

That means "You're crazy!" in Italian. Nicole wants me to teach her as many words as possible in Italian, and she's a very fast learner because she's so clever – definitely the cleverest in our group of friends.

"Right, everybody!" said Mr. Cary. "Looks like you've had a good lunchtime session. But let's have a bit of a clear-up, yes? The bell for afternoon school will be going in a minute."

He was right. And we all had to rush around tidying everything away, because the first lesson of the afternoon was PE and it's quite a way from the art room to the netball courts, and we all needed to get changed.

As we hurried off, with our school bags hanging from our shoulders and bashing against our hips, we changed the subject from the Italian evening to the bike ride that was coming up. It was Izzy who started it off.

"I can't wait till Sunday," she said. "It's going to be so cool going on an outing all together."

"Aren't we lucky that we've got two things to look forward to in this half of term!" said Sasha, who's Izzy's best friend. Then she pulled a face. "Well actually I'm not totally over the moon about the bike ride, to be honest. I mean, I used to go out on my bike quite a lot when I was younger, but I haven't done it for ages, and I can't imagine I'll be fit enough."

"You'll be fine," said Izzy. "Mrs. Mellor said we'd be stopping roughly every half-hour for a break, remember."

"Yes, they're called 'pit stops', those breaks," said Bryony, who is definitely the fittest and the most adventurous of us all. She and Emily are best friends because they both love to live outside. Oh, that's not very good English. Let me think... Yes, they both love the outdoor life – that's better. In fact, Emily's family have got a farm in Ireland, so she's used to being outside most of the time. She told us we were very honoured to have her with us in the art room at lunchtime, when she really wished she was gardening in her special patch of land behind the school kitchens where she's starting to grow vegetables. We all knew that was true but not one of us took offence, because Emily didn't mean it horribly. She just speaks her mind and we're used to it.

"I'm looking forward to the lunch on Sunday," I told the others. "I've never had a picnic indoors before!"

"I know!" squeaked Emily. "It's in a barn, isn't it? With hay bales to sit on!"

"I think it's the parents of a Year Nine girl from Beech House who own the barn," said Bryony. "Mrs. Truman said it's huge, which is lucky 'cos she also said there are about thirty of us who've signed up for the bike ride!"

"What's that?" came Mrs. Truman's voice as we went into the changing room to get ready for netball. "What did Mrs. Truman say?" she added in a pretending-to-be-strict voice.

"We were just talking about the bike ride," Sasha explained. "Are there about thirty of us going on it?"

"That's right! And mainly Year Sevens like you lot, so you'll need to be fit!" Mrs. Truman was hurrying us all up. "Get a move on now, girls!"

Get a move on. That sounds really funny to me. Like I said, I've still got a lot of English to learn!

After lessons finished for the afternoon, Nicole and I went back to Forest Ash to get our bikes from the outhouse behind it. Sasha and Izzy decided to come with us, but Bryony went off with Emily to work in her garden.

"I wish we could go off the premises," said Izzy. "I really want a proper practice, not just a ride around the Silver Spires grounds."

"It's quite a long distance if we go up the main lane and down all the side paths, though," Nicole pointed out. "And round the tennis courts and everywhere."

I knew I'd be perfectly happy to ride around the grounds here – I love every centimetre of it. "And the grounds are so beautiful," I added.

"I know. It's just that I really wanted to have a

chance to get used to riding with traffic – and obviously there's none of that here," said Izzy.

"Mrs. Truman said she'd organized a route that hardly touches main roads for Sunday," said Sasha.

But I agreed with Izzy about the traffic. I'm used to riding a bike because I've done it on holiday at our little house in the mountains ever since I was about four, but that's a really quiet place with hardly any traffic. Also, I have to remember to ride on the left-hand side of the road when I am in England.

"It must have seemed a bit weird putting your bike on the plane!" Nicole said to me, as we got our helmets on.

I nodded as I remembered how I felt when we picked it up from the special collection point in the airport. A part of me was really excited of course, but there was still a little part of me feeling sad, because this would be the first time I would be on a bike ride without my family.

In the end, the four of us rode round the Silver Spires grounds about three times and it was great fun. We didn't want to run anyone down so we couldn't go fast, because after school there are always loads of people milling about, either on their way to clubs or just…what's the phrase? Oh yes, just hanging out. I like saying that!

"What else is happening on the Italian evening, Antonia?" said Sasha, as we put our bikes away and went over to Emily's garden so the six of us could all go to supper together.

"Well, Nicole, Matron and I are going to perform a little play in Italian," I said. "We're going to mime a lot, and at the end we'll see if anyone could understand what it was about!"

Nicole's eyes widened with worry. "Only don't tell anyone about it yet, because I might be rubbish and then we'll have to abandon it."

"You won't be rubbish!" I promised her.

"No, of course you won't," said Izzy. "You're the only one from our dorm who'd ever actually be capable of doing a play in a foreign language, you know – apart from Antonia, obviously!" Then she laughed. "I can't wait to hear Matron speaking Italian. I mean, I've only ever heard her say things like hello and bye-bye, but she makes every word sound so dramatic, doesn't she?"

I couldn't help giggling, and Nicole laughed too, because Izzy was right. Matron loves learning Italian from me. In fact, she and Nicole have a kind of competition between themselves to see who can learn the most, and Matron's actually quite far behind Nicole, but her accent makes up for it.

She puts her heart into every word. So at least everyone will be looking at Matron and not me when we come to do the play on the actual evening.

"What's so funny?" came Emily's voice from the other side of the tall hedge.

But by the time we'd all gone through the gate into the garden, she'd forgotten about her question. "Look! The first row of potatoes is now in!" she announced proudly.

"And I've got it on record!" said Bryony, tapping her camera.

"What, you've taken a picture of the bare soil?" asked Sasha, looking puzzled.

"It's not bare soil!" said Emily. "It's soil with potatoes in it!"

She was staring at the ground with eager eyes as though she was waiting for the potato shoots to come pushing through at that very moment, and Bryony quickly took a picture of her just like that. Then when the rest of us started laughing, we found ourselves being photographed too.

Emily rolled her eyes. "Please excuse my friend, you lot. She's gone a bit camera mad!"

We helped Emily put her tools away in the outhouse, because it was time to set off for the dining hall, and on the way we had bets on what might be for supper. This is our latest craze. We only ever bet with sweets but it's still great if you happen to guess right and you can keep the whole handful.

"Pizza!" said Nicole. "That's my guess!"

"Yuk, hope not," said Emily.

That gave me a bit of a jolt because Mrs. Pridham had asked me to plan the food for the Italian evening and I'd already suggested pizza as the main dish. I've got some ideas for toppings from my dad and Mrs. Pridham is really happy because lots of Forest Ash girls are helping, and as we're following Papà's recipes the food will be genuinely Italian.

"I thought you liked pizza, Em?" I said.

Immediately she broke into a smile. "Oh, I do, and I know I'll love *your* pizza, Toni, because it'll have all sorts of exciting ingredients. But the ones here are always plain boring cheese and tomato."

I was relieved that I didn't have to worry about my pizza toppings, but there was something that she'd just said that had given me a bit of a surprise, and it seemed I wasn't the only one.

"What did you just call Antonia, Ems?" asked Nicole.

"Toni! Nice name, eh?" grinned Emily. "Don't know why no one's thought of it before."

"It's only nice if Antonia thinks so," said Nicole, who's always so thoughtful.

"It's what my dad calls me, actually," I said. I didn't add that I'd felt a moment of homesickness at the sound of it. I nodded slowly. "Yes...I like it."

"Hey, cool!" said Emily, rushing off ahead of us all and leaping into the air. "*I* thought of it. Good old me!" But then she came racing back a moment later. "Okay, lay your bets everyone. Nicole reckons it's pizza. I say spag bol."

"I think chicken Kiev," I quickly added. And while the others made their guesses and kept changing their minds, a picture grew in my mind of Papà in his restaurant with his tall chef's hat and his crisp white apron that somehow manages to stay nearly clean even after three hours in a hot steamy kitchen. I could just see him moving smoothly but very quickly from the cooker to the serving hatch and from the chopping board to the sink, working away without ever stopping for a second, his deep strong voice calling out urgent instructions to the other two chefs. Everyone is a little bit afraid of Papà. And that includes me. Well, I'm not exactly afraid, it's just that he seems to make all the decisions in our house. For example, it was his idea that I should come here to Silver Spires.

When he and Mamma said they had something to discuss with me after lunch one Sunday last spring, I remember how my stomach went into – what do you call it? – yes, knots. Paolo and Ricardo had gone down the road to my grandparents' house and I was planning on joining them, but Papà was looking at me with such a serious expression that I knew this was going to be something very important, and I felt scared.

"Toni," he began, tipping his head to one side. "Mamma and I have made a decision about your education. These days it is important to be able to speak English. It is the most widely spoken language in the world and opens many doors in another important world – the world of business."

"Yes I know, and I've already started learning English at primary school and next year we carry on at secondary…" I interrupted. But he put a hand up to stop me gabbling on.

"To learn English properly you need to be in a country where English is the main language spoken."

I remember how the tears had gathered in my eyes as I realized what was coming next and how I probably wouldn't be able to stop it.

"And it's not just for the sake of the language, it's also about absorbing the whole culture."

"But I don't want—"

Again he put his hand up. "We have found a wonderful school in England that you will love, Toni. A school for girls, which looks like a very happy school. I thought we could have a look online together."

"You want to send me away! I won't see you for weeks and weeks. I'll be miserable. How can you do this to me?" And with that I'd burst into tears and Mamma had tried to cuddle me and soothe me but I'd pushed her off and refused to look at the computer. So Papà printed off some pages and left them on the table for me and eventually, when both my parents had left the room, I looked at the pages. I saw lots of smiling girls and some beautiful buildings, especially one with twinkling panes of glass and tall spires that looked as though they were studded with diamonds. But so what? It was an English school with English girls, so no one would want to be my friend because they wouldn't understand me and I wouldn't understand them.

For days I felt a big weight of sadness on my shoulders and a hot fire of anger inside me that Papà could be so horrible. I asked why *me*, why not Paolo and Ricardo? But Papà said they'd be going away too when they were older. I cried and cried and kept looking at the printed pages all about Silver Spires. Sometimes I threw them down in disgust, but one time when I was looking at the sparkling spires I was tempted to look on the website and find out more. I couldn't read the English very well and that made the fire inside me rage even more. But then I realized that if I went to this school I would actually become an English speaker. And there were other pictures that Papà hadn't printed – a dormitory with laughing girls sitting on their beds, a grand theatre, a swimming pool, a place for little pets to live. And slowly, slowly I started to think I might manage. I couldn't get so far as to think I might be happy, but I thought I might manage.

And I have. I've more than managed. I more than like it.

I love it.

Chapter Two

The days leading up to the bike ride were great
fun. Those of us who had been nervous before
felt only excitement at the thought of our big
adventure. Every morning, the first one to wake up
in our dorm (which is called Emerald dorm, by the
way, because all the Year Seven dorms are named
after precious stones), would jump out of bed and
rush to the window to see what the weather was like.
It's nearly always Emily who wakes up first actually,
and she often goes for a walk before breakfast, even
when it's cold.

"How can you bear it?" I always say to her as I
hug my dressing gown around me tightly.

She looks at me as though I'm *pazza* – I mean crazy. "But it's lovely and warm!"

And that's when I realize I'm still Italian at heart, because I've never been lovely and warm in England.

When Sunday arrived I found myself singing a song Papà taught me when I was much younger, called "Cincirinella". Cincirinella was a man who had a wagon, and a mule to pull it along, and together they went trotting hundreds of kilometres over mountains and hills, sometimes in wind and rain. But they were always happy together and Cincirinella sang his trotting song as he rode along. I used to love singing that song with Papà when we rode our bikes together.

"Someone's happy!" said Miss Stevenson, the assistant housemistress, who was one of the staff coming with us on the bike ride. She's only in her early twenties and I like her very much because we have something in common. She was new at the beginning of this year too, and she felt homesick and strange just like I did. She actually once told me that, and it helped me to know I wasn't alone.

"Have a great day!" said Mrs. Pridham, who saw

us off. (We were the only six going from Forest Ash.) "And take care, all of you!" she added.

"We will!" we called out brightly and I thought how like a mother she was, waving at us with her big smile, but with eyes that also held worry. I recognized that look, because it was the same one I'd often seen in Mamma's eyes when my brothers and I were going off with Papà on a bike ride.

Miss Stevenson led our little procession to the meeting place near the main entrance of Silver Spires. There were three other teachers actually cycling with us on the trip, but I only knew one of them a little, who is called Miss Graham. Then there was Mrs. Truman and Mrs. Bradley, the matron of Beech house, who were both travelling in the school minibus with supplies of biscuits and water and plasters and towels and anything else we might need. But we'd been told that the main reason for the minibus was just in case anyone's bike got a puncture or something else wrong with it, so then both the girl and the bike could have a lift.

Eventually when everyone was present and ready, with their helmets on and jackets zipped up, we set off, and I felt so happy because the sun came out at that very moment.

"Do you think it's going to be fine all day?"

I asked Miss Stevenson, who was just in front of me in our long snake.

"The forecast is for sunshine and showers," she answered. "Antonia," she added, "I've been meaning to ask you, what's that song you were singing?"

"It's called 'Cincirinella'. Papà taught it to me when I was little. There are actions too – crazy actions!" I added, thinking of my whole family dancing and singing this song for fun last Christmas. Even Nonno and Nonna – sorry, Grandpa and Grandma – joined in.

"Hey, cool!" said Izzy from in front of Miss Stevenson. "You could teach us the actions for the Italian evening, Toni!"

"Yes, why not?" agreed Miss Stevenson, laughing. "Then we can all be crazy together!"

So after that, my five friends and Miss Stevenson all started joining in with me, trying to learn the song. The tune is simple but they had trouble with the Italian words, apart from *"Trotta, trotta, Cincirinella!"* which they sang high up – no, I mean, they sang at the tops of their voices. In English you pronounce "Cincirinella" like this: Chin-chiri-nella. Emily said she loved the sound of that word.

"You can teach us the actions when we have our first pit stop, Toni!" she added.

It still felt new and a bit strange to hear my friends calling me Toni, but I noticed that Nicole never used it.

After a while we found ourselves in a lovely quiet country road and because there was almost no traffic at all, we all started chatting, although Mrs. Truman said we must stay in single file and keep our wits about us. (I like that expression, it's funny.) Emily kept wanting to sing the "Chin song" as she called it, so there we were, riding further and further through the lovely countryside, all singing away, and it felt so strange – as though I was back in my childhood with Papà, happily riding along. But then there was a long hill that seemed to go on for ever, so we were all silent apart from our puffing breathing.

Bryony soon got ahead and it looked as though she was at the front of the whole group, which shows how fit she is. Emily wasn't far behind her, but the rest of us were much further back. When we were almost at the top, the Silver Spires minibus passed us and a smiling Mrs. Truman waved at everyone and gave us a thumbs up. It was a relief to have a downhill bit straight afterwards and then another kilometre or two of flat before the next hill. This one was not so long but it was very steep, and it was such a lovely feeling when we finally came to the top of that hill and saw the minibus parked up just ahead in a big lay-by, which had its own picnic area with two tables and benches. Mrs. Truman was standing at the entrance to the lay-by waving a bright flag over her head. "Well done!" she said as we each rode in. "Come and enjoy a nice break now. I've got biscuits and drinks here for you."

So we all propped our bikes up or just laid them on the ground, and then helped ourselves to whatever we wanted to eat. Mrs. Truman demonstrated some leg stretches and said that everyone ought to do them at each pit stop, so that nobody would be stiff the next day. We had to stand on one leg and clasp the ankle of the other leg behind, keeping our knees level, and hold the stretch for about ten seconds.

When we'd finished the stretches, us six friends went off to the far end of the lay-by so I could show the others the "Chin dance", as Emily continued to call it. I couldn't help noticing people staring at us from car windows as they drove past and it's true we must have looked quite a funny sight in our cycling gear, clapping our hands and then linking arms to spin each other round – especially Emily, because she hadn't even taken her helmet off. Bryony had brought her camera in her bike bag and she got Miss Stevenson to take a picture of us.

"It's all about timing, isn't it?" said Nicole, really getting into the dance.

"No, it's all about cycling," laughed Mrs. Truman, coming over to us at that moment. "Back on your bikes now, girls. I'll clear up here while you lot follow Miss Graham. It's about eight kilometres to the next stop, all right?"

I don't know if we got stronger as we got more used to biking a long distance, but I felt more comfortable during the second stretch, and I was almost keeping up with Bryony as we went down a lovely long hill. We were singing our hearts out, because we knew we were just coming to the barn where we would be having lunch.

"*Cincirinella l'aveva una mula…*" I sang as it started to rain very lightly.

"Didn't you say there's a bit of the song about the wind and the rain?" Nicole asked me.

I was enjoying myself so much that I sang her the bit about the weather as I tilted my face towards the raindrops.

"*…non temeva ne pioggia ne vento…*"

I heard Nicole call out something from behind me, but I was too far ahead of her and her words got lost in the wind as I sailed down the hill at top speed.

"*Trotta, trotta cantava contento!*" I carried on happily.

There was Nicole's voice again, but I didn't hear what she was saying, because I was so far in front now. And my wheels turned faster and faster as a picture of Mamma and Papà dancing with big smiles on their faces rushed through my mind.

"Antonia!"

Something was happening to me. One second I was sailing happily along, and the next it just felt too fast, but when I put the brakes on I wobbled. The words of my song seemed so far away. That terrible cry of Nicole's was the last thing I heard before...
Bang!

There were gasps and shouts and the whirring of my front wheel, but I couldn't see it. In fact, I couldn't see anything.

"Antonia! Oh no! Antonia! Say something." It was Nicole's voice, softer now and full of crying.

But I couldn't speak. I couldn't open my eyes. I could only screw up my face as a searing pain shot down my leg, and then another and another, until the pain was constant. And my shoulder hurt too, and my arm and my hand. They were stinging. I kept my eyes closed as though it might block out the pain, but then I felt another kind of pain. The pain of the realization that I'd ruined the day for everyone, because I could hear Miss Stevenson and

Miss Graham and the other teachers all shouting out instructions to the rest of the girls to get off the road and stay with their bikes.

"I know it's a very quiet road, but just in case there happens to be any traffic."

I wondered then whether *I* was off the road. I wasn't sure exactly where I'd fallen, but I didn't want to open my eyes to see. The next thing I heard was Miss Graham saying that she'd call an ambulance and a second later Miss Stevenson's voice was right beside me.

"Keep perfectly still, Antonia," she said. "Can you hear me all right?"

I licked my lips and swallowed. "I..."

"What's hurting?"

I felt her press something on my hand and raised my head just enough to catch a glimpse of a screwed-up tissue.

"Stay still, Antonia, it's only a bit of blood. Now keep talking to me. Tell me what's hurting most. Is it your leg?"

I wondered why she wanted me to keep talking, but I thought I ought to do as I was told. "Yes, my leg...sorry..." I couldn't help starting to cry.

"No need to say sorry. No need at all. Look, here's Mrs. Truman."

"I've got a pillow and a blanket from the van," said Mrs. Truman, crouching down beside Miss Stevenson and sounding puffed out, as though she'd been running.

"She's moved her head already, so that's good," Miss Stevenson said quietly.

"You don't feel any pain in your neck?" asked Mrs. Truman.

"No." I could hardly speak, my leg was hurting so much.

"The ambulance should be here at any moment."

"I need an ambulance?" I opened my eyes and saw the worry on Mrs. Truman's face, then saw her try to hide it.

"Just to be on the safe side."

On the safe side. I closed my eyes again and felt myself break into shivers.

"Thank goodness it's stopped raining," murmured Miss Stevenson.

"But her clothes must be damp," said Mrs. Truman, reaching for my hand as I winced with the pain from my leg. "Oh dear, hang on, more tissues needed here." She turned to Miss Stevenson. "Emma, can you get me cotton wool and the bandage with the antiseptic wound pad on it from the first aid kit."

I was wondering what Mrs. Truman wanted it for until I looked at my hand and saw that the tissue she'd pressed onto the bottom of my thumb was soaked with blood, and that blood was running down my wrist too. At the same time I felt a hand on my shoulder and turned my head slightly to see Nicole's wide eyes, and behind her everyone else standing like statues with their bikes and their anxious faces. "You were going really fast and you hit a bit of a pothole or something," said Nicole. "You've grazed yourself quite badly on your shoulder and your arm...and your hand."

"Grazed?" I didn't think I'd ever heard that word before.

"Cut the skin... And..." I saw her glance towards Mrs. Truman before she said the next few words. "...You might have broken something. Are you... feeling...okay, though?"

Poor Nicole was crying too. I had to quickly reassure her I was fine, even though I wasn't really, as the pain in the lower part of my leg was the worst pain I'd ever felt. "I'm in..." What was the word? "...agony." Maybe if I sat up a bit I'd feel better. I was really careful not to jolt my leg even the smallest amount, but still there were pains that shot up and down from my knee to my foot, and

Mrs. Truman told me again to stay still.

"I've got my coat in the van if you'd like a bit of extra warmth."

"It's okay, it's just my leg..."

But it wasn't just my leg. I realized my shoulder and my arm were stinging and I knew they'd probably be bleeding, because I must have scraped them when I'd fallen.

Miss Graham suddenly stepped forwards and spoke gently. "Shall we get out of the way if the ambulance is coming, Mrs. Truman?"

Mrs. Truman had got the bandage in place over my thumb and around my wrist and the bottom of my hand, and was just tying the knot. She stood up and I could hear her talking quietly with Miss Graham, about who would stay with me, and all the arrangements for the rest of the day. It seemed that Mrs. Truman herself was needed to drive the minibus, but Miss Stevenson would stay with me. Then Miss Graham turned and called out instructions to the girls, but her voice seemed too loud because everyone was already silent.

A moment later she leaned over to talk to me. "We didn't want to move on until we were sure you were definitely all right, Antonia." She smiled at me and the smile carried on around the rest of the girls.

"Right, the ambulance will be here any moment so I think we'll make tracks. Follow me, girls. Let's go and find this barn, shall we?" She was trying to sound all bright, but I felt terrible because I really felt sure now that I'd ruined everyone's day. Miss Graham's voice turned gentle one last time as she spoke to me. "Next time we see you, you'll be feeling a million times better, you know!"

The girls were moving off with their bikes but Nicole didn't move a muscle. "I'm staying with you, Antonia."

"No, it's okay, you don't want to miss the barn and the lunch and everything," I said in a gabble, because she'd get left behind if she didn't go quickly.

"I want to stay with you," she answered simply, just before a great swishing surge of bicycle tyres and voices started up all around me.

"Glad you're okay, Toni," said Emily, holding her bike awkwardly and trying to bob down in front of me. "We'll be thinking about you."

"And Nicole will tell us how you're getting on," said Bryony.

Then Sasha and Izzy both blew me kisses.

"See you soon, Antonia."

"You'll be better in no time."

And as they cycled off behind the others, from somewhere in the distance I heard the ambulance siren wailing.

The lovely ambulance people gave me a painkiller but it didn't take effect straight away. It hurt when they examined my leg.

"Looks like it's definitely a fracture," said the kind man in a green uniform.

Miss Stevenson and Nicole travelled in the back of the ambulance. Nicole was closest to my head and kept whispering things to me as though it might hurt me if she spoke any louder. "They're worried you might have concussion," she explained after the ambulance man shone a tiny torch light into my eye.

"Just checking your pupil response to light," he told me. It was strange because he was quite the opposite to Nicole and spoke in a loud voice, as though I might not be able to hear properly as well as everything else that seemed to be wrong with me.

"Right, that seems to be fine. Let's check out these cuts and grazes," he then said, moving my hair very carefully.

It turned out that I'd scraped some skin off my shoulder and the top of my arm, but the man told me it was nothing serious. "Just needs a bit of dressing here and there," he said. And the fold of skin under his chin wobbled the tiniest bit as he flicked his head to look at my hand. "Someone's made a neat job of this bandage." He nodded. "Mmm. Excellent."

It suddenly struck me that I was noticing everything in such detail. Nicole's soft voice, the man's loud voice and wobbly chin, the different rooftops that I glimpsed through the ambulance's blacked-out windows. My whole world was crystal clear, and right in the middle of it was my throbbing leg and a feeling of helplessness that made me want to cry. And then a few tears did squeeze their way out of my eyes and rolled down the sides of my face. Nicole asked the ambulance man for a tissue and I dabbed at my cheeks, feeling silly and babyish. But then I saw that Nicole had tears in her eyes too, so I stopped thinking about myself for a few seconds, until another wave of pain hit me.

Chapter Three

"It hurts quite a lot," I told the doctor in the hospital through clenched teeth, wishing desperately that I could have something stronger to make the pain go away.

"We'll get you straight in for an X-ray," he said, looking down at me carefully. "Apart from your leg, how do you feel, Antonia?"

I told him I thought I was all right, but I didn't tell him I hated lying on this stretcher bed because I felt so helpless. Then I had to give lots of details about myself, like what I was allergic to and what history of illness there was in my family, and halfway through I realized that Mrs. Pridham was right beside me. She reached for my hand – the one that didn't have the bandage – and held it tight, which made me want to cry again. But I didn't.

"You'll soon feel better now, Antonia," she said, nodding and smiling an anxious smile.

I nodded back and I heard Miss Stevenson telling Mrs. Pridham about my accident as I was wheeled away.

"See you in a minute, Antonia!" Nicole called after me.

And suddenly I thought of loads of questions I should have asked and I couldn't think why I hadn't asked them ages ago. Like, was my bike very badly damaged? Did I lose consciousness at all? What exactly happened when I hit the pothole? Was it my fault that I'd fallen off? How long would I have to stay in this hospital? Was it far from school? Would Mrs. Pridham stay with me? Would Nicole be allowed to visit me? And then I gasped as I thought of the biggest question of all. Did my parents know what had happened to me?

The X-rays showed that my head was fine and I didn't have concussion, but my tibia – which they also called my shin bone – was broken in my right leg.

"Unfortunately the bone is out of alignment," the nurse explained. "Tell me if you want me to slow down or explain anything," she added, which was kind of her.

"Er...can you tell me if my parents know what has happened to me?"

"Yes, I'm sure they will have been told." She smiled. "We'll ask your housemistress about that, shall we?"

I felt better then, so I could go back to my other questions.

"Yes...what is...alignment, please?"

"It means that the two bones will need to be pulled together in an operation under general anaesthetic. You won't feel a single thing of course. Then the plaster cast will be put on."

Not feeling a single thing sounded wonderful at that moment. "When will I have the operation?" I asked quietly.

"First thing in the morning, dear. I'm afraid the operating theatres are all in use until then."

I breathed in very deeply then let out my breath heavily, because I so wanted to start to get better and for everything to go back to normal. The nurse must have known what I was thinking. "The time will go more quickly than you think, dear. I'll get you settled in the ward, and I've got another painkiller here to top you up."

That was a relief because the other one didn't seem to have made much difference.

"And when I've had the operation will I be allowed home?"

The nurse frowned and there was a little pause. "Home? You mean back to your school?"

"Yes, back home...to school," I said.

She smiled then – I mean a really big wide smile – before her face turned grave again. "Well, you might be ready to go by tomorrow afternoon. But we usually keep patients in overnight when they've had a general anaesthetic. Let's just see how you get on, shall we, and cross that bridge when we come to it."

I liked that expression, and even in my pain I repeated it to myself, so I could try to remember it and write it down later.

"So just one or two nights on your own, Antonia," said Nicole, when the nurse took me back to her and Mrs. Pridham a bit later. "And we can phone each other and text, can't we...?" She turned to the nurse. "Is that allowed?"

"Yes, but we ask patients to think about others. It's important that no one is disturbed."

"Will Antonia have a TV?" asked Nicole.

"Yes, you'll need to buy a card for that," said the nurse.

"I'll get you a card," said Mrs. Pridham immediately, "and look..." She held up a bag that she'd been clutching. "I've brought you your long pink-and-white T-shirt and your cardigan so you'll feel a bit more at home. I put your pyjamas and toothbrush in too, just in case, so you don't need to worry about that. And the most important news is that we've told your parents, and they're flying over! They'll be here this evening, and I'll stay with you until they arrive."

Something inside me seemed to burst suddenly into song. I felt so happy. "My parents are coming here to the hospital?"

"Yes, I thought you'd be pleased," said Mrs. Pridham.

Then there were even more questions whizzing round my head. Who exactly had Mrs. Pridham spoken to on the phone, my dad or my mum? And what did they say? Were they upset? And what about Papà's work? How could he leave so quickly? But I couldn't ask my questions, because I was being wheeled away to the ward and Nicole was walking along beside me with Mrs. Pridham just behind.

"I'm allowed to stay too, for now," said Nicole. "I've got to go back for supper, though. Miss Stevenson's coming to collect me at half past five."

I nodded and felt my eyes closing. What time did Nicole say? Five o'clock? And what time was it now? I tried to raise my wrist to look at my watch, but I really was too sleepy. I just didn't seem to be able to keep my eyes open.

When I woke up, the first person I saw was Nicole. She was reading a newspaper, which I didn't think I'd ever seen her do before. That was the only thought I had before a little surge of pain in my leg made me gasp and remember all that had happened.

Nicole leaped out of the chair, dropping the newspaper on the floor. "Are you okay?"

I tried to focus. "How long have I been asleep?"

She looked at her watch. "Well it's four thirty right now."

"Oh, ages!" I suddenly felt really guilty. Poor Nicole must have been so bored waiting for me to wake up. "Is Mrs. Pridham still here?"

"Yes, she's gone for some fresh air. We've been taking it in turns."

"Oh, thank you…"

"Are you hungry or thirsty? Shall I get the nurse?"

"I'm not really hungry. I wonder when I'll be allowed more painkillers…"

"Oh, poor Antonia. It must be awful."

"No, poor you. You've missed the picnic lunch and everything. I've really messed up your day, haven't I?"

"I don't mind about that. I just keep remembering the moment when you came off your bike. You hit the ground so hard and then rolled over. But then you were completely still and silent and I thought… I mean…I was so scared…what might have happened to you."

"Poor Nicole," I said, reaching for her hand. "Well I'm okay now, see?" I tried to smile, but it must have come out like a horrible grimace because another wave of pain shot through me at that moment.

"Oh hello, Antonia," said a nurse – a different one – coming in. "How are you feeling after your sleep?"

"Can I have another painkiller?"

She took something off the end of my bed and started to read it. "Just looking at your notes... Yes, you can." She glanced at her watch. "In a few minutes, all right?"

Suddenly, Miss Stevenson appeared at my bedside and Nicole turned big accusing eyes on her. "I thought you said five thirty!"

"Yes, I know I'm a bit early," said Miss Stevenson, looking very surprised. I was surprised too. I'd never heard Nicole sound upset like this. "But I've got to get back on duty, I'm afraid. Matron was having the weekend off but when she heard the news she insisted on coming back to help cover for Mrs. Pridham, only her train was cancelled so she's going to be late."

Nicole bit her lip and looked down, and I felt awful for causing everyone so much trouble.

"It's all my fault for going too quickly down that hill," I said, as more tears gathered in my eyes.

Miss Stevenson shook her head. "No it's not. These things happen. Don't start blaming yourself. It's nobody's fault. The important thing is to get you better."

"What time do you think Antonia will be able to come back to school tomorrow?" Nicole asked the nurse.

"Well, she's down to have the op at half past eight so there's a tiny chance she might be able to come home the same day, but it depends on how she reacts to the anaesthetic as to whether she comes home later that day or not till the day after."

"You can text me to let me know," said Nicole.

"Aha, you've woken up!" came Mrs. Pridham's voice from the doorway. "You're looking better already, Antonia." She smiled. "I've forgotten about the TV card. I'll just go and sort that out now." Then off she went again.

"Now, here's a bag with some more things that Sasha's sorted out for you," said Miss Stevenson, taking some bits and pieces out and putting them in the little cabinet beside my bed. "Look, she even thought to pack the book you're reading at the moment."

"Good old Sasha." Nicole smiled. Then she bit her lip again. "See you tomorrow, Antonia."

"Yes, see you tomorrow all plastered up!" said Miss Stevenson, putting a hand on Nicole's shoulder to guide her away.

I watched Nicole right until she got to the door, where she turned to give me a wave. I knew she'd do that and I was ready to wave back and was pleased because my shoulder and arm and hand didn't hurt at all. So at least I'd only got my leg to worry about now. I so hoped my operation would go well and that I could go back to school the same day. But I knew there was no point in thinking about that now. It only made me anxious. I'd just have to cross that bridge when I came to it. I smiled to myself for remembering the new expression I'd learned. Then I smiled again – a bigger smile – because soon Mamma and Papà would be with me.

"Oh darling, we're so happy to see you!" said Mamma, in Italian, of course.

I guessed she must have said that at least twenty times since she and Papà had arrived, and I gave her another hug because I was really, really happy too. From the moment I'd found myself lying at the roadside several hours earlier, everything had felt like a dream, and this was the most dreamlike part of it all, because my parents were actually here in this country, in this hospital. They'd asked me over and over again about the bike ride and the accident and they always finished off by saying, "*Non importa. Siamo qui adesso e tutto andrà benissimo.*" ("Never mind. We're here now and everything's going to be all right.")

I wanted to hear about my brothers and what was going on back home though. "So Ricardo and Paolo are with Nonna and Nonno?"

"*Si, si,* they are having fun with their grandparents!" Mamma laughed.

I looked at Papà. It was odd to see him so… strained. He'd spent ages talking to Mrs. Pridham when they'd first arrived, and though they were talking very quietly and had their backs to me, while Mamma kept hugging me and asking me loads of questions, I'd managed to pick up a few words of Papà's, like "helmet" and "ambulance" and "first aid", and I knew he'd be wanting every detail from Mrs. Pridham.

But at least now he was smiling. "We must book into a hotel, *cara*," he said to Mamma. *Cara* isn't her name. It's Italian for "darling". Then he turned to me. "The nurse told us we could only stay a short time with you this evening, but we'll be back tomorrow first thing before your operation."

"We were lucky that they let us come in at all!" said Mamma. "Visiting time was over a long time ago."

"But of course they knew these were special circumstances," Papà put in. He smiled again, but I could see sadness in his eyes. "We came as soon as we possibly could."

"So little time to organize everything," said Mamma. "We couldn't have done it without Nonna to have your brothers, and Nonno to drive us to the airport."

"Thank goodness there was a plane with spare seats on it leaving so soon," said Papà. "Otherwise..."

His voice trailed off and he raised his hands in a gesture of helplessness. It was so unusual to see my father like this.

"I'm sorry, I'm going to have to ask you to leave now," said the nurse, arriving at that moment and talking quietly because some people in the ward were already asleep.

Mamma's English isn't all that good so she wasn't sure what the nurse had said and had to get Papà to translate. Then she gave me another hug and lots of kisses while Papà asked the nurse what time they should arrive in the morning. She thought eight o'clock would be the best time so they could sign the consent forms.

"Sleep well, Toni," said Papà.

"Yes," said Mamma, blowing me another kiss as they went off. "*Ti amo, cara*."

That means "I love you" in Italian, and I could still hear the words long after they'd both gone and

I was left lying there, in a ward full of people and yet feeling so alone. I found myself thinking about Emerald dorm and my friends. They might be asleep by now, or maybe still reading with their night lights on, or talking. I wondered if it felt funny in the dorm with my empty bed. If only I could phone Nicole to have another chat. But it was too late now. She would have handed her phone in to Matron, like we have to every night.

Then I wondered whether Nicole was missing me. In a way I hoped she was. But that was the lonely part of me. The other part of me wasn't so selfish and liked to think that she was fast asleep dreaming lovely dreams.

And that's what I would do too. I closed my eyes and tried to ignore the throbbing in my leg.

Chapter Four

The next morning I was woken really early by lots of noises – people talking, nurses wheeling trolleys and things around, curtain rings jangling along their railings, the chink of cups, the rattle of spoons. My eyes were wide open and I was ready for action. This was the day that I was having my operation.

I didn't feel at all nervous, just happy that the pain, which I could still feel despite all the painkillers I'd had, wouldn't last much longer. And also excited that soon I'd be able to act like a normal person again – well, fairly normal, apart from a plastered leg and a pair of crutches. But then I wondered if I'd need a wheelchair to help me get around at school. No, surely crutches would be fine. I imagined myself leaning on them while all my friends signed my plaster cast. It would be fun to see how many signatures would actually fit onto it. I'd start by asking everyone in Forest Ash.

Mamma and Papà were definitely surprised to see what a good mood I was in when they arrived. I think they'd been expecting to see me anxious and quiet, but actually they were the ones being anxious and quiet, and Mamma grew even more anxious when the doctor came to explain the operation. She had to keep asking Papà to translate and it all sounded very serious, talking about realigning the bones and making sure that they were set in exactly the right position.

The nurse took the dressing off my hand and I couldn't believe what a mess it looked on the fleshy part of my palm at the bottom of my thumb, and right across the inside of my wrist and up my arm. I hadn't been able to bring myself to look at it when the doctor had checked it the day before. Now the nurse dabbed at it with antiseptic from a bottle, which stung, and then she put a different dressing back on. "It would have needed stitches if someone hadn't got that wound pad on so quickly," she said, looking grave.

"My teacher bandaged it up straight away."

"Well, she knew what she was doing." The nurse nodded her approval.

Even as I was being wheeled into the anaesthetic room I still felt happy, and another nurse said she didn't think she'd ever seen anyone go in for an operation in quite such a jolly mood. "I think I'd like to give you a job here talking to all the patients and cheering them up!" she joked. "A happy patient gets well much more quickly."

It felt so strange waking up in my bed in the ward. I didn't know where I was at first, but then I saw Mamma, and everything slowly fell into place.

"There!" she said, clapping her hands together dramatically as though I was a little girl again. "There!" she repeated. "All done!"

I looked down at my leg. It was covered from just below my knee to my foot in a thick white plaster. I'd seen these casts on other kids at primary school occasionally, but this was the first one I'd ever had myself.

I looked at my watch. It said twelve fifty. "Wow! That was a long operation!"

Mamma laughed. "It wasn't so long. Don't you remember waking up in the recovery room?"

I shook my head.

"Yes, I spoke to you there and you seemed wide awake. They checked that everything was fine, then brought you back here. But the nurse told us that patients often drop back to sleep afterwards, and that's exactly what you did!"

I suddenly realized that Papà wasn't with us and was about to ask where he was, but Mamma must have seen my eyes flicking around.

"Papà is...on the phone. He will only be—" She broke into a smile. "Oh, he's here!"

I looked over to see Papà striding across the ward and noticed his face light up when he saw I was awake. But there was something a bit impatient in his eyes too and I wondered whether he was worrying about his work back home in Italy. I changed my mind about that a few minutes later, though, because he sat down in a chair and started talking to me with smiling eyes. "The operation was a great success, Toni. Your leg has been X-rayed and the bone looks perfectly aligned. Once the plaster is off, you'll be good as new!"

I think he was trying to cheer me up by talking about when I'd be all better. He probably thought

I was dreading the thought of spending ages not being able to walk without the help of crutches, but I didn't actually mind. All I wanted was to get back to school.

Only then something struck me. "How long does my leg have to stay in plaster?" I asked the nurse, who had just arrived to ask me if I wanted to go to the loo and have a wash.

"Six weeks," she answered.

I did a quick calculation. Six weeks would take us up to the last week of the Easter holidays. So I'd be in Italy. "Oh, so will I need to finish my holiday early and come back here to have it taken off?" I asked Papà. "Or can we go to a hospital in Italy?"

"Er..." He and Mamma exchanged a look and Papà quickly explained to Mamma what the nurse had said.

"Don't worry," said the nurse, "you can have the cast taken off anywhere. We wouldn't expect you to come back here specially if you're abroad. You just go to your doctor and he will refer you to the orthopaedic clinic. But before that you'll need your plaster checking for fit in a week or two." She smiled at me. "Sometimes when the swelling goes down the plaster feels a bit loose."

I saw Mamma and Papà exchange another look as

Papà translated what the nurse had said.

Then Papà went off for a little walk while Mamma helped me get washed and dressed, which made me feel so much better.

It surprised me when the nurse asked if I wanted some lunch, because it felt as though I'd only just had the operation and it was still early in the morning, but of course quite a few hours had gone by and I'd had a big sleep since then. I said I thought I could manage a little bit, but as soon as I started eating I felt sick and Papà had to rush and get the nurse to bring me a bowl.

"Have a little rest," said the nurse. Then she turned to Papà and I heard her say something about how patients are sometimes affected by the general anaesthetic in this way and that it would probably be best to keep me in for the night so they could check up on me.

But I was impatient to get back to my friends. "I'm feeling much better now I've been sick," I quickly told Papà. "Honestly."

Papà nodded and patted my hand, but he didn't look convinced. Then Mamma put the TV on, only I must have drifted off to sleep straight away because I've no memory of whatever we watched.

* * *

It was much later when I woke up, and at first I couldn't remember where I was. Then I saw Mamma and Papà by my bed and it all came flooding back to me.

"Feeling better, Toni?" Papà asked me straight away.

I nodded and sat up. Yes, I really was feeling better. In fact, my mind went straight to Silver Spires and whether I would be able to get back to my friends.

"Maybe you would like a walk around?" said Mamma. "Papà can ask the nurse if there is a wheelchair. Look, here she comes now..."

My thoughts rushed ahead. I knew I'd have to get used to walking around on crutches, so why not straight away? "Er...could I try walking with crutches?" I asked the nurse.

"Well, the physio will be giving you a session on the crutches some time before you go, but it's early days at the moment. Let's give it a bit more time, shall we?"

A wave of disappointment hit me. Time was running away and soon this day would have disappeared completely. But the nurse was getting me a wheelchair, so there was nothing I could do. Or perhaps there was. Yes, I would show her just how much better I felt by leaping out of bed quickly and hopping to the wheelchair. That would surely convince her.

So that's what I did. But I didn't get very far. No sooner had I swung my legs out of bed than I felt dizzy and had to look down, clutching my head in my hands.

"Oh my goodness!" said Mamma. "You're so pale, *cara*!"

There was a sharp edge to Papà's voice. "You need to take things gently, Toni. It takes time to get your strength back after an operation."

The nurse crouched down and looked up at me as I sat shakily on the side of my bed. "Are you feeling a bit queasy, Antonia?"

I'd never heard the word "queasy" before but I could guess what it meant.

"A bit."

"Your body is still recovering from the anaesthetic. Look, the doctor's coming round now. Let's see what he thinks, shall we?" She scribbled something on the notes at the end of my bed, then hurried away, but she was back by the time the doctor got to my bed.

"So how's the leg, Antonia? No pain now?" he asked me.

I hesitated. There was a bit of pain, but it was nothing compared to how it had been before. "It's fine, thank you."

He smiled and gave me the same careful look that the nurse had given me. "But you've had some sickness and dizziness?"

"Yes, just...a bit."

He turned to the nurse. "I think she should stay at least another night to be on the safe side."

At *least* another night? This was getting worse with each passing minute. I'd been so looking forward to going back to Silver Spires today, but now it looked as though even tomorrow was doubtful. The doctor was heading off to the next bed, so I knew I had to be quick if I was to manage to get him to change his mind. "If I'm fine tomorrow morning, will I be able to go home?" I asked him in a gabble.

"Well that depends on the circumstances at home," he said, turning round and giving me what I would call a searching look. "You'll need someone looking after you all the time for a few days at least. It's tougher than you think managing with one leg out of action. Have you got lots of stairs, for example?"

I thought about Forest Ash and my heart started to sink. "Well—"

"There are lots of stairs, doctor," Papà interrupted in a calm voice. "It's a boarding school." Then he turned to me. "Antonia, it's much more sensible to stay overnight as you've not been feeling well, and then we'll see about tomorrow."

The doctor smiled at my father and nodded. "That's right, Antonia. Let's get you in the right state before we throw you out, eh?" He gave a little chuckle and, with another smile at my parents, turned to the patient in the next bed.

The nurse helped me back into bed and I flopped back against the pillows, feeling *abbatutta*. I don't know how to say this word in English, but it's like being tired and depressed.

Later, though, after Mamma and Papà had gone and I was on my own, I tried swinging my legs out of bed again, and this time I didn't have any dizziness. Maybe Papà had been right about it taking time to get my strength back. I was definitely getting better now and I felt sure I would be ready to go back to my friends tomorrow.

Thinking about Nicole and the others reminded me that I hadn't looked at my mobile all day. It was such a good surprise when I found loads of texts. All my friends and Miss Stevenson and Mrs. Pridham and Matron had wished me luck with the operation and then there was a later text from Nicole saying she guessed I'd be all plastered up and ready to go back to school by now and she couldn't wait to see me.

I quickly replied to tell Nicole the bad news, but I promised her I'd definitely be back the next day. Then I flopped back on my pillow again, determined to save every drop of strength so that nothing would stop me leaving hospital at the earliest possible opportunity.

"Right, take your time now, Antonia." The physio was supporting me as I got the crutches in place under my arms. "Now, try a few steps along the corridor."

It was ten o'clock in the morning, the day after my operation, and I felt a lot better. The nurses couldn't believe the improvement I'd made, so they'd happily agreed to letting me try out the crutches.

"Excellent!" said the physio, because I found it easy and had gone halfway down the corridor and back. "Now for the stairs. They're a bit trickier."

And they were, especially as I had to be careful to hold the right-hand crutch in a particular way, so it didn't hurt my hand. But still I managed, and afterwards, when we went back to the ward and met up with my parents, the physio told Mamma and Papà that I was a "natural".

"So why don't we go and have a drink at the café," said Mamma, "to celebrate?"

But I was desperate to get ready to go back to school. All we were waiting for was to see the doctor one final time, and the nurse had told us she was certain he'd let me go when he saw how much better I was.

"I'm not really hungry or thirsty, Mamma. Shall I pack my things together?"

Mamma turned anxious eyes to Papà and I felt confused for a moment. What was there to be anxious about now I was better? Or was she worried about how I'd manage on crutches at school?

"When I get home to Silver Spires, I'll have loads of people to help me carry things, won't I?" I said in my brightest voice to try and reassure Mamma. Then I couldn't help a giggle spluttering out. "Isn't it funny the way I keep saying 'home'? I suppose it's because school *is* my home in term time. And of course there's always someone on duty, like Matron or Mrs. Pridham. They can help with—"

"Antonia, we need to talk."

I got a shock at those words of Papà's, because

they'd come out so strongly and seriously, and he hadn't called me Toni. There was something in his tone that reminded me of the time last spring in Italy when he'd first mentioned Silver Spires. And why was Mamma looking down? What did we need to talk about? Whatever was the matter? Mamma sat on the edge of my bed and Papà sat in the chair next to it.

"So perhaps we should go to the café?" he said more calmly.

I shook my head and he sighed.

"Antonia, your mother and I have made a decision."

My mouth felt suddenly dry and I sipped at the water on my trolley as my father kept talking.

"We didn't want to say anything until you felt well again, but this whole experience has made one thing quite clear to us. It was such a shock when we heard the news that you'd had a bad accident on your bike. We felt so worried and so powerless and helpless with the enormous distance between your school and our home. And I can't tell you how difficult and complicated it was to make this journey to England at such short notice to be with our precious daughter, which was all we wanted to do..."

He paused and my heart pounded and pounded with fear and yet I didn't know what there was to fear.

"...So we are taking you back home with us to Italy."

I swallowed. His voice and his face were too grave for the words that had just come out of his mouth. I wasn't sure what he meant. Or was it that I *was* sure but I couldn't face it? My voice shook as I asked the question that had found its way from my racing mind to my mouth. And my insides trembled with dread at what his answer would be.

"Do you mean you're taking me home early for the holidays or..." It was no good I couldn't say the rest of the sentence.

"No, we're taking you out of Silver Spires altogether. It's for the best."

My heart stopped pounding and squeezed with misery.

Chapter Five

For the first time in my life I was about to cross a line with my father. I was going to question his decision, because it was stupid and just…wrong.

I raised my voice. "You can't do this to me!"

Mamma quickly pulled the curtains round the bed and told me to be calm.

"How can I be calm? You're making me cross. It was you two who wanted me to come to Silver Spires in the first place. You said I had to improve my English…"

"Yes, you're right," said Papà. "And that job is now done. You speak English wonderfully well.

Better than we had hoped for."

I wished I hadn't said anything about English now.

"But it's more than just the language. It's the whole…culture. That's what you said. I remember." I felt close to tears, because I didn't have enough arguments. Not ones that Papà would listen to anyway. This had to be a terrible dream that I was about to wake up from.

He was nodding. "Yes, I agree that culture takes a while to absorb, but you have had a good taste of it." Then he sighed. "Look, Toni, we know how much you love your school, and if it were in Italy then everything would be fine. But it is simply too far away. Your mother and I had no idea what it would be like if you had an accident or an illness. That was short-sighted of us. But now with all this…" He held up his hands and cast his eyes around the ward. "…It's frightened us. It's changed our view. We can't take the risk of something like this happening again. You need to be with us in Italy to recuperate."

I tried not to shout. "But I can recuperate at Silver Spires! Or even if I recuperate in Italy, why can't I come back to Silver Spires next term?" I knew I was sounding desperate, but that was because I *was* desperate. "I mean, think about it, what if you two were both away on business and I was at a school in Italy and I had a terrible accident? You'd still have a great long journey to make."

"We have all the family in Italy, Toni. Nonno and Nonna, your uncles and aunties. There will always be someone to look after you. We are a close-knit family. We look after each other. That's what families are about."

I didn't know what to say to that so I just stared at him, and the look I got back said, *I'm not changing my mind*. But surely he didn't understand how important Silver Spires was to me.

"My school is like my home, Papà!" I said, raising my voice again.

"Yes, it is a very caring community, I agree," he said calmly.

"And what about my friends? What about Nicole, my best friend? I can't leave Nicole."

"Nicole and your other friends can come to visit us in Italy, *cara*," said Mamma in her gentle voice.

"It's not the same. The friendship won't be the same if I only see them once a year or something. I don't want to lose Nicole." I could feel myself getting close to tears.

"You won't lose Nicole, but you will gain other friends," said Mamma.

"We'll find you another perfect school in Italy," said Papà.

I felt myself kind of shutting down. I wanted to block my ears like I did when I was a child and an older boy in the playground used to tease me with talk of slimy frogs and toads because he knew it made me feel ill. I hung my head.

I didn't care about any stupid Italian schools. All I cared about was Silver Spires.

"We know it's hard to make changes," said Mamma, "especially big ones like switching schools. But once you've got used to the idea you'll be fine, because although you can't see it now, it's all for the best."

"Best for *you*. Not for me," I said flatly.

"No, we're thinking about all of us, but especially you." Mamma reached for my hand. "You were happy to have us here with you yesterday when it was your operation, weren't you?"

I nodded forlornly, because that much was true. I *had* been pleased to see them. Obviously. They're my parents.

Papà suddenly stood up and spoke briskly. "We have an appointment to see Ms. Carmichael and Mrs. Pridham now, Toni. We've already explained our feelings briefly to Ms. Carmichael, but there are things to finalize."

"You have to give a term's notice anyway, so you can't just take me straight away!" I said in a bit of a screechy panic.

"We're going to pay for the term," said Papà firmly, "but you won't be staying to complete it. I'm sorry, Toni, the decision is made, and one day you'll realize it *is* for the best, even though, as Mamma says, you can't see it now."

He paused and gave me a kind look, but I couldn't take a kind look from such an unkind person so I looked away and listened to his horrible words going on and on.

"By the time we're back, hopefully the doctor will have seen you and we'll collect you and take you back to the hotel. You're not allowed to fly for at least two weeks, so we've booked the train for Thursday. That will give us time to get all your things from school packed and you'll able to say goodbye to your friends…"

My eyes filled with tears and Mamma gave me a tight hug, then stood up. "We won't be long, *cara*," she said in a shaky voice, as Papà beckoned the nurse over and had a quick word with her, which I couldn't hear. "I'm sure you'll feel pleased when you're used to the idea."

My father bent to give me a kiss but I didn't

move at all. I just stared straight ahead.

Then they were gone. I pulled the top pillow from behind me and flopped back on the bed, the pillow over my face to stifle my sobs.

From somewhere outside my horrible tear-soaked world I heard the soft voice of one of the nurses.

"Antonia? Phone, dear. Are you awake?"

My eyes were open in a flash.

"It's your friend, Nicole." She was handing me a hospital phone. At the sound of Nicole's name I felt like crying all over again. How ever was I going to tell her the terrible news?

"Hi."

The nurse smiled and walked quickly away with silent footsteps.

"Hi, Antonia! I got the ward phone number from Mrs. Pridham, because you didn't answer your mobile."

"Oh sorry...I didn't...hear it ring."

"Have you got your crutches?" she went on, excitedly. "When will you be back?"

I swallowed. "Something terrible has happened."

There was a gasp, then I heard her repeat my

words in an anxious whisper. The others must have been standing round.

"What, Antonia? Are you okay? Whatever's happened?"

"My dad is taking me out of Silver Spires." My throat started hurting.

Her voice sounded suddenly very small. "What do you mean, taking you out?"

"For ever. He and Mamma are on their way to see Mrs. Pridham and Ms. Carmichael right now. They don't want me to come back to school, because they feel too far away from me in Italy now that this accident has happened."

I started crying then and from the other end of the phone I could hear Nicole whispering the news to the others in the very fastest gabble, and in the background Emily was saying something, but I couldn't tell what. Then Nicole was back with me again, sounding as though she was in tears herself.

"That's absolutely awful. What are we going to do?"

"There's nothing we *can* do. He's made his mind up."

"So...aren't you coming back here at all...?"

This was the worst conversation I'd ever had to have with anyone. "I've got to stay at their hotel tonight. Then tomorrow my parents are planning to bring me back to school to collect all my stuff. Papà's booked the train for Thursday as I'm not allowed to fly. There's nothing we can do." I dissolved into tears.

But Nicole sounded suddenly stronger. "We can't do *nothing*. We have to make him change his mind. And Emily says what about the Chin song and the whole Italian evening this Saturday? You can't miss that. You're the main person."

I'd completely forgotten about the Italian evening. It didn't seem very important compared to everything else that was happening. But wait a minute... Emily was right. I was supposed to be in charge of the food and the play and the song. I'd been hoping to teach the actions to everyone in the whole house. How could I miss the Italian evening? An idea was starting to form in my head. It wasn't a brilliant one, but it was the best I could come up with, and it might work.

"Nicole, listen..."

"Yes..."

"You need to get to Mrs. Pridham before Papà does," I told her urgently.

"Y-yes..." she said more hesitantly.

"And ask her if she can tell my dad how important the Italian evening is..."

"Yes, that's a good idea. If he'd just let you stay for that…"

"It would give us a bit of time together… Only, make sure you remind her how much I'm supposed to be doing for the evening, like the food and the play and everything…"

"Yes, and then she'll realize you have to be at school with me and Matron to rehearse… Otherwise your parents might say you can stay till the weekend as long as you're in the hotel with them."

My heart sank like a stone when Nicole said that. It was no good. Even if a miracle happened and Papà agreed that I could stay till the weekend, he was sure to book me into the hotel with them so I wouldn't have to cope with all the stairs and everything at Silver Spires. And I couldn't bear to be so near to Silver Spires and yet not actually there.

"I've just had another thought!" said Nicole. "Maybe Mrs. Pridham could invite your dad to do the cooking at the Italian evening! He's a proper chef, after all."

Why hadn't I thought of that? "That's a brilliant idea, Nicole. Then he'd feel really involved and also it would be rude to turn down an invitation like that from Mrs. Pridham."

"I'll go and speak to her right now," said Nicole.

"Surely she'll be able to persuade your dad to let you stay here till the weekend." Nicole's voice started to go very quiet. "Then at least we'd have a few days…"

I swallowed, thinking that all we were doing was stretching out the agony and making it even harder to say goodbye afterwards. And anyway, Mrs. Pridham would probably agree with Papà that the hotel idea was much more sensible. Why would she want to be bothered with someone on crutches in her boarding house with all those stairs, when there were lifts at hotels and my parents had come all the way from Italy?

"Okay," I said, feeling my voice fading out with hopelessness. "Phone me back when you've spoken to her."

As soon as I'd rung off from talking to Nicole I gave the phone back to the nurse. Then I switched on the TV and stared at the screen, but I didn't see anything at all because I was so taken up with my thoughts.

It gave me a shock when my mobile suddenly started vibrating and the name *Nicole* appeared on the little screen. I hadn't expected her to call back so soon. I quickly grabbed the phone, but in my hurry I knocked my bandaged hand against the chest of drawers beside the bed, and felt a sharp pain.

"Hi, Nicole," I said in a worried whisper. "What happened?"

As Nicole talked, I watched my white bandage turn smudgy pink with the blood seeping through from where I'd knocked my hand, and I tried to ignore the throbbing pain. If only I'd been a bit more careful – now there was something else for Papà and Mamma to fuss about.

"Well the moment Mrs. Pridham opened her door I burst into tears," began Nicole, "and poured it all out to her about your dad taking you away on Thursday and everything. I could tell she was quite shocked. She said she was due to see your parents in half an hour but she had no idea that they had made a definite decision, or that they'd be taking you away so soon. So then I started begging her to invite them to the Italian evening, and her eyes were really flicking sideways all the time and she was wearing a gigantic frown as though she was trying to work out what to do."

"So did she agree to invite them?"

"She told me she'd have to wait and see what your parents had to say first, and that if they'd made up their minds to remove you from school immediately there might not be anything she could do about it. But she did say that she had your welfare at heart and that she hoped she might be able to persuade them at least to stay on till Saturday, because it's only a few days and the Italian evening would be a lovely send-off for you." Nicole sighed. "And that was all really, except that she said I should try not to worry, and that she'd come and find me later."

"And did you say about me staying at school and not at the hotel?"

"Yes…no…did I?" Nicole sounded all flustered and upset. "No, I forgot. Oh, I'm so stupid… It was just that she was hurrying me away, because she said she'd just been on the phone for ages before I knocked at the door and she had stuff to do before the meeting. So I had to go."

"Don't worry. At least you said about the Italian evening."

There was a silence, then Nicole said, "Oh, by the way, Emily says she's going to kill your dad."

And I don't know if it was the flat way she said it, or the whole ridiculous situation we were in, but I burst out laughing and then Nicole was laughing too and we couldn't speak for ages.

"You'll phone me as soon as Mrs. Pridham speaks to you, won't you?" I said eventually.

"Yes, of course I will."

"I'd better go. The nurse is giving me funny looks. Perhaps I'm disturbing people."

"Okay, bye, Antonia."

"Bye."

The nurse wasn't giving me any funny looks really. How could she? The curtains were still pulled round my bed. It was just that there was nothing left to say and I didn't know how to finish the call. I'd been laughing my head off a minute before, but now all I wanted was to pull the pillow back over my face and cry. Except that even that seemed too much effort.

"Ready for a cup of tea, hon?"

A new nurse, a really young-looking one, had poked her head through the curtain, and all I could see was her smiling face.

"Erm...yes please." I was hanging on to my tears so they didn't fall out, but it was making my throat hurt.

"Are you all right, honey?"

I nodded, not trusting myself to speak.

She came inside the curtain then and pulled it back closed, and quickly glanced at my medical notes. "Antonia – that's a pretty name."

I tried to smile but it didn't work.

"Rossi. That's not English, is it?" she went on.

"I'm from Italy," I said flatly.

"Aha!" She sat down on the chair by my bed and drew it up closer to where I was perched on the edge, my plastered leg stretched out on the bedclothes. "I heard you laughing a moment ago. On the phone, were you?"

I nodded. "It was my best friend. Sorry, I hope I wasn't disturbing anyone."

"No, not at all. I only heard you laugh. You must have a nice quiet telephone voice. Anyway...best friend? That's nice." Then her eyes widened. "Oh! Have you been on the phone to Italy? That'll cost you a bit!"

"No, I go to Silver Spires boarding school here." And as soon as I said it, I realized it wasn't quite true what I'd said. "I mean, that's where I went until... now."

That was when I started crying, and I felt so stupid and embarrassed, especially when the nurse had only just heard me laughing. She must have thought I was really strange.

She took my hand and noticed the bloodstain on the bandage. "Oh dear. I'll sort that out for you. But listen, hon, if you want to talk, I'm here."

"It's just that my dad..." I managed to say

between little sobby breaths, "...is going to take me away from my school and I don't want to leave... My parents want me closer to them...not stuck in England when they're in Italy..."

"Well, that's understandable. It's because they love you so much."

"Yes, but they're taking me straight away and not even letting me stay till Saturday for the Italian evening at school, unless Mrs. Pridham – that's my housemistress – persuades them to let me."

"Right..." The nurse looked as though she was searching for something to say but couldn't think of anything. She probably didn't understand what on earth I was talking about.

"They've got an appointment to see her right now...then they're coming back here and I'll find out the worst."

"Or you might find out the best. I'll go and get you that tea, hon, and a fresh dressing for your hand, and let's hope for the best, eh?"

By three o'clock I was in such a state. I'd been trying to read my book, but I felt so tired all the time. The kind nurse encouraged me to lie down properly in the bed and have a sleep.

"A general anaesthetic really takes it out of you, you know, hon, and –" her voice softened – "I think you've had a bit of a setback with the news you've had, too."

I did as I was told and lay there, tense and knotted. But exactly the same thing happened that had happened the day before. My tension must have somehow slipped into tiredness, and when I woke up I was shocked to realize I'd been asleep and even more shocked to see Mamma and Papà there.

"Hello, *cara*!"

The knots came straight back into my stomach as I remembered the awfulness of the news I'd had earlier. I searched my parents' faces for any sign of what they were about to say now.

"How are you?" asked Papà.

"I'm okay. How…did the meeting go?"

"Everything is sorted out," said Mamma. "Ms. Carmichael and Mrs. Pridham were full of praise for you. They're so sorry to be losing you, of course, but they completely understand why."

Now there was a big stone crushing the knots, squashing them so I couldn't feel them any more, but weighing my spirits down with its heaviness.

"Mrs. Pridham talked about the Italian evening, Toni," said Papà, and I saw a little gleam in his eye and felt the tiniest ray of hope. "She asked me if I would do some cooking." Papà chuckled, but it seemed like the kind of chuckle you might do if you thought something was ridiculous, so then the stone pressed harder, flattening my spirits even more.

"We didn't know about the Italian evening until Mrs. Pridham mentioned it," said Mamma, "and we both thought what a lovely goodbye it would be for you. So Papà would be happy to cook and you'll be pleased to hear we've changed the train booking to Sunday."

Everything lightened inside me. "Oh, that's great!" I sat myself up a bit straighter, and out of the corner of my eye I saw the nurse who'd been so kind to me hovering nearby. Maybe she was wondering how I was getting on. I wasn't really sure myself, as there was one important thing I still had to know, and I was dreading the answer.

"Did…Mrs. Pridham…tell you what *I'm* supposed to be doing at the Italian evening?"

"Yes, she explained that you have quite an important role," said Papà.

"And that you have to practise your play," Mamma added.

I swallowed and waited. The nurse was waiting too. When I flicked my eyes to the right I could see her at the nurses' station, standing quite still and looking directly at me.

"Mrs. Pridham seems to think you'll be able to manage at school until the weekend," said Papà. He shook his head slowly. "I can't say we're over the moon about it, because you'd be so much safer in the hotel with us." Then he shrugged. "But apparently it's not the first time someone at Forest Ash has broken a leg."

"So...I'm allowed to go back to Silver Spires?"

"We've agreed to let you stay there till Sunday morning, yes. Our train is at three twenty. And, Antonia..." Papà's eyes were boring into mine. I swallowed. "We're not changing our minds. You do understand that, don't you?"

That last bit was awful. But at least I wasn't going immediately. I had five more nights at Silver Spires in Emerald dorm with my friends. That was something.

I subtly nodded at the kind nurse and she gave me a big thumbs-up sign.

Which made me smile inside.

Chapter Six

"**R**ight girls, you're free to go," said Miss Stevenson at the end of Tuesday evening's prep.

"Yay!" said Emily. "Can I go outside, Miss Stevenson?"

"Just for a few minutes then."

"Let's practise the Chin dance!" said Izzy. "Come and sing for us, Toni."

But I wasn't really ready to go yet. Ever since I'd arrived back at Silver Spires just two hours earlier, I'd found myself short of time. First I'd gone straight to my dorm, and seen that there was a mattress on the floor near my desk with all my bedclothes on it. Mrs. Pridham told me this would be easier for me than trying to climb up my ladder to bed, and I felt quite excited about sleeping on the floor. It looked very cosy. Then, while my friends had gone to supper, I'd unpacked my things and Mrs. Pridham had brought me some sandwiches and a mug of hot chocolate. I'd missed the whole day's lessons, of course, and even though Mrs. Pridham said I didn't have to worry, I'd decided to come to prep to try and catch up with as much as I could. But the session seemed to be over so quickly, and I'd still got quite a bit of copying to do.

"I just want to finish this history," I said, as everyone started to leave the prep room. "Is it okay if I stay for a while, Miss Stevenson?"

She gave me a really sympathetic look, as though she was sorry for me having to spend extra time catching up with the work I'd been missing while I was in hospital.

"I don't mind, honestly," I said, smiling at her brightly. And I really didn't. The only thing that was a bit annoying was trying to write with my hand bandaged up. If only it had been my left hand, everything would have been so much easier.

I looked at the clean white dressing which the

kind nurse at the hospital had put on earlier. She'd told Mrs. Pridham that it should be changed again the next day and Matron had already told me she'd do it tomorrow and that in the meantime I should keep it completely dry. She said the drier it was, the faster it would heal, and she thought I must have cut it on a sharp stone or something because it was quite a deep wound. I couldn't wait till I could get the bandage off completely, but I guessed that would be a few days away still.

As I settled down to carry on copying up Nicole's history, I noticed that she'd got a book out of her bag and I realized she was planning on staying with me.

"I'll be fine. Really," I told her. "I'll see you up in the dorm."

And that was when I saw that she was giving me that same sympathetic look that Miss Stevenson had given me earlier.

"What?" I asked, turning from her to Miss Stevenson.

"Nothing," said Nicole. "I don't mind waiting for you, honestly. It's too hard to carry stuff with your crutches and everything."

She was right. It's actually impossible to carry anything when you've got crutches, because you need both hands for them, and even a shoulder strap can easily slip off. "Oh thanks, Nicole."

Miss Stevenson was still sitting at her desk at the front, which was ridiculous because I didn't need her to stay to supervise me.

"We're okay on our own, Miss Stevenson."

She just nodded and went out, but I couldn't get the sad look on her face out of my mind as I carried on copying up Nicole's notes. And it wasn't until I was coming to the end that I realized something amazingly obvious. Something that Nicole and Miss Stevenson must have already thought of.

I looked at Nicole, who was silently reading beside me, frowning at the page in a world of her own. "Why am I bothering with this?" I asked in a flat voice. "It's pointless, isn't it? I won't need it at my new school, will I? All the work will be completely different there. I won't even be writing in English." I felt such emptiness at that moment that I didn't even have the energy to get up from my seat.

Nicole sighed and shut her book. "Let's not think about that," she said, trying to force brightness into her voice. "Let's try and enjoy ourselves until the weekend. That's what we said we'd do."

I felt even sadder then, and it was a good job Emily came in at that moment.

"We're stuck!" she announced, standing at the

door with her hands on her hips. "We're still outside, trying to work out what comes after this bit…" It was so funny seeing her standing in the doorway then, with her arms flinging out all over the place as she half sang, half spoke the same few words of the song over and over again.

Then Bryony appeared. "Actually Miss Stevenson's sent us in now, Ems, 'cos she's going to lock up soon. So we're going to the common room. Hurry up, you two."

"Come on, Antonia," said Nicole, grabbing my bag as well as her own and slinging them both over her shoulder.

Nicole held open the door and I walked into the common room. It was the first time I'd been in there since I got back from hospital, and immediately I felt like a celebrity, because loads of people came rushing over and asked if they could sign my cast. So far only the girls from my dorm and a few other Year Sevens from Forest Ash had signed it, but these were older girls – Year Eights and Nines. I lay down on the sofa with my leg up and let them sign away.

"Don't press on it too hard," said Nicole, looking anxious. "It would be terrible if anything happened to

Antonia's leg. The bone's been realigned, you know."

It was sweet the way she was being so protective. And I was glad she'd said something, because it *would* be absolutely terrible if anything else happened to my leg. Papà would – what's the expression Bryony sometimes uses? – yes, *he'd blow a fuse* if anything went wrong with my recuperation while I was at Silver Spires. He'd probably change his mind about the Italian evening and change the train booking so we would have to go home immediately. I hated having thoughts like this and I pushed them away so I couldn't sink into sadness again, as I watched my cast filling up with messages.

Some girls just wrote things like *Get well soon!* But others had written funny messages, and a Year Ten called Tabitha, who's really good at art, drew a picture of me on crutches. I don't know how she managed to make it look so realistic.

"Right, that's enough for today!" said Nicole, putting her hands up and nodding her head firmly.

"Yes, because we haven't done the dance yet," said Izzy.

"What dance?" asked Tabitha.

"One that Antonia taught us before she came off her bike," Emily explained. "We're going to do it at the Italian evening. It's called the Chin Chirie song."

"*Cincirinella!*" chorused the rest of us.

"Actually the Chin Chirie song sounds much better!" laughed Tabitha's friend, Sarah. "Come on then, show us how it goes. Then we can *all* do it at the Italian evening."

So I sat down in a chair and showed them the arm movements, while Nicole stood in front of me and did the skips and turns, and we all sang the song at the same time. "Brilliant!" I said, clapping my hands together like a little child.

"Year Sevens, time to get ready for bed!" came Matron's bird voice. (That's what I call it, anyway, because Matron always sounds as though she's singing when she talks – all bright and bubbly. I think the word that Nicole uses is "chirping" or "chirruping".)

We didn't really feel like going up to bed because we were having such a good time, but as we left the common room Izzy said, "Let's get ready really quickly, then we can carry on in the dorm."

As it happened, though, we didn't have time, because with my bad hand as well as my leg, everything takes me so long to do. Cleaning my teeth is awkward and so is washing my face – well, washing any single bit of me actually.

I was the last one back to the dorm from the

bathroom and as I slowly pushed open the door I heard a loud, "Ssh, Emily!" and noticed that everyone was suddenly silent and Nicole had gone a bit red.

"Were you talking about me?" I asked, instantly feeling a bit upset.

It was Sasha who answered. "Yes, but nothing... much."

"What, though?" I couldn't help my curiosity when they all seemed to be acting rather mysteriously.

"We can't tell you. It's a secret," blurted out Nicole.

I felt my stomach do a backflip. I wasn't used to my friends having secrets from me. It was obvious it must be something about me leaving, but I couldn't work out what.

"You'll see," said Nicole, putting her arm round me a bit awkwardly as I propped my crutches against my chair.

I nodded to show that I was fine with the secret, even though I still felt a bit shaky inside, and then I went over to the bed that I'd been given. It was going to feel very odd sleeping in an ordinary bed on the floor when I was used to our lovely cabin beds that all the Year Seven dorms have at Silver Spires, but it was true I'd find it too difficult to climb up the ladder to my usual bed.

"You look funny down there, Toni!" said Emily, looking at me from her own bed.

"You look funny up there!" I replied, which made everyone laugh for some reason. I pretended I found it funny too, but inside I felt that heavy weight of sadness pulling me down again.

"Right, give me your phones," said Izzy.

In our dorm we've made a little rota for handing in our mobiles to Matron each night, and this week it was Izzy's turn. As I pulled my duvet over my plastered leg and watched her go off with the six phones, I was taken back to that time in the hospital when my leg was throbbing and I couldn't even talk to Nicole because she would have handed her mobile in.

For a moment I felt as though I'd been standing in shallow seawater with a boiling hot sun beating down on me and now a lovely wave of relief was flooding over me that I was back here in the dorm with my friends. But a second later it was as though the sun had gone behind a dark cloud and I was standing there shivering and alone. How was I going to feel back home in Italy, night after night, without Nicole and the others and this life I've come to love so much? I'd have my family of course, but would there always be a part of me looking back sadly to my short happy time at a very special English boarding school?

After tonight there were only four more nights to go. I looked across at Nicole. She was lying perfectly still staring up at the ceiling. I wondered if she was having the same thoughts as me. And that made me so sad, I doubted I'd ever get to sleep.

By the end of morning lessons on Wednesday I was exhausted. It's impossible to explain what it's like going round on crutches from lesson to lesson. Stairs are the hardest thing to manage and I kept on wishing I could go faster, because I was holding Nicole and the others back. They were totally kind and understanding, carrying stuff for me all the time and holding open doors and everything, but still it wasn't easy. And the other problem was my hand. I had to hold the crutch on my right-hand side really carefully to make sure I wasn't putting too much pressure on my hand and hurting it. So I was always stopping to adjust my grip, which was annoying.

At lunchtime Sasha took my crutches to stand them in the corner of the dining hall once I was safely sitting on the bench. Then Nicole brought me my main course, and Emily poured out my water to save me lifting the jug with my bandaged hand. Izzy took my main course plate away and brought me dessert, and Nicole finally cleared that away again, while Bryony went to get my crutches.

"I bet it will be a relief when I've gone and you don't all have to wait on me any more," I said, as Nicole pulled out the bench so I could swing my leg over to get out.

Emily laughed and said, "Don't be silly, Your Majesty, we love waiting on you," which made the others laugh too. But I noticed Nicole was looking down, and that gave me another jab of sadness, though it was my own fault for saying what I said. I just wasn't thinking.

"Let's go and get on with our masks," said Sasha, looking anxiously at Nicole. "Mine's nearly done, Antonia. Izzy and I did loads on Monday lunchtime."

It seemed to take ages to get to the art block, even though I was swinging myself along as fast as possible and really trying to be speedy on the stairs. Quite a few other Forest Ash girls passed us on the way, because everyone was keen to get their masks done now Saturday was drawing so near.

I could feel myself actually sweating by the time I was sitting down at the art table. I wished I could stand up and dart around or reach out to get the paint and things I needed like the others were doing, but it was impossible with my leg out of action and my hand only half working. So I had to just sit there while Nicole waited on me again.

After a while, though, I really got into painting the last tiny bit of my mask and only spilled one splodge of purple on my bandage. Then I pushed the elastic through the holes I'd made in the sides of the mask, and Nicole knotted it for me, because it was too fiddly for my bandaged hand. She did her own too and we proudly showed each other our finished products.

Izzy and Sasha tried not to look but they couldn't help themselves, so in the end we all showed each other our masks, although we tried to keep them hidden from the other Forest Ashers who were in the room. Emily's mask still wasn't finished, because it was so big and she was painting it to look like a massive butterfly. Personally, I liked hers the best.

"My mum told me that she'd heard on the news that British butterflies were in danger of becoming extinct," she explained, "so I thought I'd make one that would last for ever!"

Bryony had her camera with her because she seemed to take it around with her all the time nowadays, and she took a close-up of Emily's mask and then decided to photograph all the masks. Mr. Cary came in when she was doing that and as usual he insisted that we cleared up thoroughly before the bell went.

"Oh, I meant to ask you," he said, turning to Nicole, "how have you been getting on with—"

"Sssh!" came the voices of my five friends in one big wave.

"Whoops, sorry!" said Mr. Cary, looking a bit embarrassed as he glanced at me.

"Just ignore Mr. Cary!" said Emily.

"Absolutely! Just ignore me!" Mr. Cary laughed. "After all, I'm only the art teacher!"

"I don't understand," I said quietly, feeling that same awful feeling that I'd had in the dorm last night, as though my friends were already getting ready for the time when I wouldn't be there any more.

"You'll see on Saturday," said Nicole.

"Yes, and you'll like it, don't worry," added Emily. "It was my idea, by the way."

I smiled at her, not feeling so alone any more.

"But if you don't like it," she added, "it was Bryony's idea!"

Bryony just rolled her eyes.

Good old Emily. It's hard not to be happy when she's around.

* * *

It was PE in the afternoon and I just had to sit and watch, which was boring. Stupidly, I'd forgotten to put something to read in my bag, so I played a few games on my mobile and then Mrs. Truman said it was okay for me to go back to Forest Ash, otherwise I'd catch cold just watching. She checked I was all right to go in on my own and I assured her I was.

On the way my mobile vibrated, and surprisingly it was Papà. I stopped still and leaned on one crutch while I spoke to him.

"Mamma's just reminded me that you might be back in lessons, Toni!" he said. "But you're answering the phone so it must still be your lunch break. How are you managing?"

"It's PE at the moment so I'm..." I was about to say "I'm a bit bored", but I know what Papà's like and I didn't want him coming over from the hotel to collect me or anything like that, so I had to think quickly. "...I'm in the library reading."

"Poor old Toni! I bet you'll be glad when you can lead a normal life again."

Instead of answering, I asked Papà what he and Mamma had been doing.

"We're actually in London at the moment in a

French restaurant, having coffee at the end of a delicious meal."

So I needn't have worried about him coming to collect me after all.

"I bet the food wasn't as good as your cooking!"

Papà laughed, but the laughter seemed to dry up very quickly. "Antonia…" My stomach turned over as a memory of the last time he'd called me by my full name flew into my mind. This was something serious. Surely he couldn't have changed his mind about the Italian evening. I swallowed and waited. "…I need to come to school tomorrow to tie up some paperwork with the school office, and I wanted to check you have started to pack. Mamma and I have made a list of things we must remember, like your bike…"

Mamma had told me when they'd dropped me off the afternoon before that she didn't want me to leave my packing until the last minute, and now it looked as though Papà was coming to check up on me. The trouble was, I hadn't even started yet, because even the thought of packing made me feel like crying.

"I…I won't forget anything…"

"All right. I'll see you later. I will take the chance to look at the cooking facilities while I'm there."

I felt much happier talking about cooking than packing. "I think you'll like the kitchen, Papà. And everyone is really looking forward to tasting your food!"

"And how are you managing with your crutches and the bandage on your hand?"

I looked down at the bandage. It had pink on it again because I'd knocked my hand earlier on, but it was only a gentle knock, thank goodness. "My hand's fine, and I'm getting really fast on my crutches."

Papà chuckled. "Well done!" Then I heard Mamma's voice in the background and knew she'd be wanting to talk to me.

"Hello, *cara*," she said in a bright voice when Papà handed her the phone. "Are you getting excited about Saturday evening?"

Was I? I wasn't sure that *excited* was quite the right word.

"Yes…it'll be great."

We talked a bit about London and then Mamma said she'd better let me go.

"Papà will see you tomorrow then, *cara*," were her last words before we rang off.

Tomorrow. Another day closer to my last day at Silver Spires.

I shivered.

Chapter Seven

After lunch on Thursday, Emily, Bryony, Sasha and Izzy went off excitedly to the art room again, even though they'd actually finished their masks completely, so I wasn't sure what was going on. Nicole and I went to Forest Ash to practise our play with Matron.

"*Buon giorno, Signorina!*" she said, when we appeared at the door to her room. "*Andiamo in la sala common.*"

I had to laugh. She'd used a mixture of English and Italian-with-a-totally-over-the-top-accent to say, "Hello, Miss. Let's go to the common room."

Actually it's difficult to translate *Signorina* properly, because in England you don't really use the word "Miss" very much, but in Italy it's quite usual to say "*Signorina*". I like the way languages are all so different. I think I'd be interested in doing something connected with languages for a career when I'm older.

As I had that thought I also had another thought – a much more important one, and I couldn't resist telling Nicole straight away. I didn't really mind that Matron was listening too, because she's so lovely and friendly and not like a proper teacher, or even like Mrs. Pridham or Miss Stevenson. She reminds me a bit of a younger version of Nonna, my grandmother, in fact.

"I've just had a great idea, Nicole!"

"Wow! It must be good, you look so happy about it!" said Nicole. "I hope you're not planning on changing the play, because I know my part now and I'd never be able to learn any more lines."

"*Neanch'io!*" said Matron. Then she burst into her little-bird laughter. "Did I get that right, Antonia? That means 'Me neither', doesn't it?"

"Yes, it does!"

"You're getting so good at Italian, Matron!" said Nicole.

"I know, but…" Matron's smiling face dropped as her sentence faded away. I guessed she was about to say, *But how am I going to manage when you've left?* Or something like that.

"Let me tell you my idea," I quickly said. "I love languages so much that I'm going to tell Papà that my biggest ambition is to be an interpreter, and for that job you need the best, *best* English, so he *can't* make me leave Silver Spires!"

Nicole was frowning thoughtfully. "It *might* work," she said slowly.

But Matron looked doubtful.

We hardly ever call Matron by her real name. But somehow I wanted to at the moment. "What do *you* think, Miss Callow?"

She pursed her lips and looked up at the ceiling as though she was trying to find the answer to my question up there. "It's worth a try, dear." She sighed, then repeated the words in a thin voice. "It's worth a try."

"But your dad would take more notice if he heard it from a teacher, wouldn't he?" said Nicole. "What about Mrs. Stockton? She could tell him how brilliant you are at English."

"That's a great idea, Nicole. I could ask Mrs. Stockton if she'd mind having a word with Papà…

as long as she really *does* think I'm good at English."

"Course she does. And we've got English just before morning break tomorrow, haven't we? You could talk to her at the end of the lesson."

"Right, that's settled then," said Matron. I could tell she was trying to go back to her usual chirrupy self, but her voice had lost its bubbles. And it was no wonder. She was probably thinking that my great idea was stupid. Even if I *did* talk to Mrs. Stockton and even if she *did* then talk to my dad, he wouldn't suddenly completely change everything just because of one conversation, would he? I don't think anyone's mum or dad would do that, but especially not *my* dad.

We practised the play for about half an hour. I was playing the part of a receptionist, so it was okay for me to sit down nearly the whole way through, thank goodness.

When it was time for me and Nicole to go off to afternoon lessons, I thought Matron looked a bit sad again, but then she caught me looking at her and immediately smiled. "I'm just thinking, Antonia," she said, "you know there are always summer school courses here at Silver Spires. If you and Nicole came along to one of those, you'd get a whole three weeks together."

I liked that thought in one way. But in another way it was a bit depressing.

"Matron obviously doesn't think it's going to do any good asking Mrs. Stockton to talk to my dad," I said to Nicole as we got to the bottom of the stairs, "or she wouldn't have mentioned summer school."

"But she might be wrong about Mrs. Stockton," said Nicole. "And it's important that you leave no stone unturned."

"No...stone...unturned," I repeated slowly. "I think I understand what that means."

"Ah, that was good timing! I was just coming to find you." We turned to see Mrs. Pridham coming out of her flat. "Your father has just phoned, Antonia. He's coming along to see the bursar to sort out the fees after school and he's popping in here first. He wanted you to make a start on your packing, so I've asked Mr. Monk to get your cases out of the storage room and take them up to Emerald. I think your dad would like to pop in and check the kitchen facilities too for Saturday night. Now the thing is, I've got a meeting after school, so once I've had a quick word with your dad, I'll leave you to show him the Forest Ash kitchen. So can you be as quick as possible coming back here at the end of lessons, all right?"

I hated all this talk of bursars and fees and it felt weird to think of Papà suddenly coming to school at the end of an ordinary day and me showing him the kitchen. But then everything was strange and different at the moment.

"Yes...that's fine. Thank you, Mrs. Pridham."

The last lesson of the day was double art.

"It's like we *live* in the art rooms!" said Emily, as we all trooped in, and Bryony took my crutches and propped them up in the corner while I hopped to my place.

I gave Emily a questioning look but she just grinned at me and said, "And no comment from you, young lady!" in a strict teacher's voice, which made everyone laugh.

When we were all sitting down, Mr. Cary started explaining about the art lesson and it was then that I noticed my bandage was starting to look rather grubby – I mean, apart from having purple paint on it. Matron was supposed to be changing it after school and I was really hoping that she might say the skin had healed enough to leave the dressing off altogether. I was so fed up with the bulky thing making everything awkward for my right hand. And suddenly I was desperate to see how the skin was doing under the dressing. There was no harm in having a quick look, was there? After all, I could get Nicole to put it back on again for me afterwards.

As Mr. Cary talked I found myself examining the knot of the bandage in my lap. It had actually come a bit loose. With my eyes fixed attentively on Mr. Cary so no one could tell what I was doing under the table, I very carefully rubbed at the knot with the thumb and forefinger of my left hand until I could get hold of one end and gently undo it.

It was at the very moment Mr. Cary told us to set to work that I found I'd unwound the dressing right down to the big wound pad, which was pressed against the fleshy bottom part of my thumb and inside of my wrist. I gave the gentlest of tugs to see if there was any dried blood sticking the pad to my flesh and it came away quite easily.

"Nicole…" I whispered, as I stuffed the bandage in my pocket with my left hand. "Look!"

She followed my eyes and looked at the hand in my lap. "Oh wow! You've taken it off. Let's see." She examined it carefully – no one was paying attention because they were all busily collecting materials they needed, and Mr. Cary was right at the other end of the room. "Does it hurt?"

"It feels fine. I think I might keep the dressing off – it's so much easier."

"But it still looks like an actual wound though, doesn't it?" said Nicole, wrinkling her nose. "What if you knock it or something?"

"I'll be really careful."

Izzy and Sasha wanted to know what we were looking at and then Emily and Bryony tuned in too.

"It must have been really painful when you first did it," said Sasha, pulling a bit of a face as they all stared at my hand.

I thought back to the bike ride and the awful moment when I realized I'd had an accident. "I can only really remember that tissue all covered in blood and the pains shooting up my leg."

"Aren't you going to put the bandage back on again?" asked Izzy, looking shocked as I got up to go and find the paper I wanted.

"No, I think I'll be all right."

Izzy looked a bit doubtful, but then we all forgot about my hand because Mr. Cary was coming over to see what we'd planned to do.

That art lesson turned out to be brilliant. Mr. Cary had collected a massive bag of freshly mown grass and split it up into about twenty smaller bags. He'd kept the bags in all different places, so some of it had dried out quickly and was really crisp and some had dried out naturally so it was soft and light, some still felt strong and supple, and some had started to go into a bit of a mulch.

Mr. Cary wanted us to make landscape pictures using the grass. But we were allowed to use it in other completely different ways if we liked. My idea was to actually drop lots of grass into the different coloured paints in my palette and create a textured rainbow effect, so I carefully took grass from each of the bags, using my left hand. Other people concentrated on just a single texture and used a lot of glue, so it was clear that everyone's pictures were going to come out completely differently.

I didn't want the lesson to end as it was such good fun, and when the bell went it gave me a jump, partly because I was absorbed in what I was doing, but partly because I suddenly remembered that my dad would be arriving at school very soon.

As we cleared away I was very careful not to bash my hand at all, and after a while I got quite confident about it and felt sure that Matron would agree that it was fine to leave it open to the air from now on. The others said they wanted to stay on for a little while in the art room – something to do with my surprise, whatever it was – but Nicole said she'd come with me. I felt sorry for her always having to stay with me when I bet she'd rather be doing whatever the surprise was, so I told her I'd manage on my own, as there were always plenty of people around to open doors and things.

"Why don't you set off, Antonia," suggested Emily, "and I'll catch you up in a couple of minutes? I'm coming over to Forest Ash to get changed for gardening."

"If you're sure you're okay, I'll stay for now and catch you up later too," said Nicole. "I just want to see something."

She took my school bag off me so I'd have nothing to carry, and off I went. But as soon as I took the first few steps I realized that my hand would need to have a plaster or some sort of dressing on it for a bit longer because it stung when I gripped my crutches. The bandage was still in my pocket but I'd never be able to put it back on again properly on my own, and anyway, the pain wasn't too bad to put up with for now, so I just kept going. I'd be seeing Matron in a few minutes, after all, before going to meet Papà, so there was no need to worry.

By the time I got to Forest Ash, though, my hand was really hurting me and I so regretted taking the bandage off. But I forgot all about that instantly when I noticed a big shiny car parked just outside the front door and wondered if it was Papà's. I'd never even thought to ask him if he and Mamma had hired a car or if they were getting around by taxi and train.

And at the same time I realized I'd got grass all down my front, so I leaned one of the crutches against the wall near the front door, and flicked the blades of grass off my sweatshirt. Then as I looked down I saw that there were also bits stuck to my plaster. If Papà saw me in this state he'd think I couldn't look after myself properly, or I'd fallen over or something. So I bent right down, balancing on my good leg, and rubbed at my plaster. Immediately I felt a stinging sensation and realized that I'd forgotten to be gentle with my right hand. I'd used it just as though it wasn't injured at all.

I drew my breath in sharply at the pain I felt, then got a shock when I saw that the skin was all broken and droplets of blood were oozing out from all over the torn area. But worse, there was quite a bit of blood on my plaster. I quickly got a tissue out of my pocket and dabbed the plaster and then regretted it instantly because now I'd made a big pink smear.

This was awful. I needed to get to a wash basin as quickly as possible.

"Antonia!"

I turned to see Nicole and Emily flying towards me.

"Is that your dad's car?" called Emily.

I didn't answer because all my attention was taken up with my bloody plaster and my hand, which looked almost as bad as when I'd first fallen off my bike. Well, it probably wasn't that bad, but my dad hadn't seen how bad it was then so he'd think it was truly awful now.

"What's up, Antonia? Did you fall?" came Nicole's voice, full of worry.

By this time they were almost right up to me and I watched the shock come into their eyes at the state of my hand and my cast.

"Oh no!" gasped Emily. "What happened?"

"Nothing. I mean, I was just rubbing the grass off me and my hand started bleeding..."

Nicole was biting her lip. "Oh, Antonia, we need to sort you out. But *is* that your dad's car?"

"That's the trouble. I don't actually know. But I'm crossing my fingers that it isn't. I don't want him to see me in this state. He'd go mad."

"It must be him," Emily pointed out logically. "We don't usually have strange cars parked outside, do we?"

"Look, I'll go in first and see if he's around," said Nicole, taking charge. "With a bit of luck he'll be in with Mrs. Pridham. I'll come out and get you as soon as I know he's nowhere in sight, then we can go straight up to Matron for a new dressing."

So Emily and I waited nervously outside and a few seconds later Nicole beckoned me in. "No sign of him. Hurry though. Remember Mrs. Pridham said she'd got a meeting to go to, so we might not have much time."

Once inside the big reception hall, Emily suggested it would be quicker to go straight to the downstairs toilets. My hand was hurting too much to manage crutches, so I gave them to Emily and just hopped across the hall towards the corridor, with Nicole helping by holding tight to my arm and sort of jumping me along. I could feel myself getting hotter with the worry of having to rush, and I couldn't wait to get to the basin and clean away the blood and get my bandage back on again.

"Well done," said Nicole, trying to encourage me when we were on the other side of the hall. "Nearly there." Then she must have seen the funny side of what we were doing, because she broke into giggles. "Sorry, Antonia, it's just that you look such a sight!"

Emily joined in and their laughter was infectious, or maybe I was just getting hysterical. "Stop it, you two! I can't hop when I'm giggling."

But a moment later the giggles froze inside me at the sound of a door opening behind us and Papà's cheerful voice.

"Ah, there she is!"

Chapter Eight

Nicole turned to me in horror as we all three stood glued to the ground like statues, not daring to turn right round.

"Lovely to talk to you again, Mr. Rossi," said Mrs. Pridham, sounding relieved. "I'll leave you in Antonia's capable hands. Sorry I have to rush off."

"Not a problem," said my dad. And I knew I absolutely had to turn round now.

I swallowed and was about to face the shock and the anger that I knew I'd see in my father's eyes, when I realized Matron was coming downstairs.

I also knew immediately that she'd seen what a state I was in.

"Ah, Antonia, there you are," she said, much more briskly than usual. "Well done for getting here so promptly." She hurried down the last few stairs and took the crutches from Emily. "I've just got two minutes to change that dressing, so could you come..." Then she looked across at my dad and spoke as though she'd only just noticed him. "Oh hello, Mr. Rossi. I'm so sorry to drag Antonia away. We'll be very quick." Her eyes came back and rested on Emily. "Could you look after Mr. Rossi, Emily? Show him the kitchen, dear, and we'll be with you in a jiffy."

It had all happened in seconds and I still hadn't turned round, but Emily was obeying Matron's instructions and Mrs. Pridham was calling out, "See you on Saturday then, Mr. Rossi."

With Matron's hand on my back I had the courage to quickly call over my shoulder, "See you in a minute, Papà," and he smiled and nodded, then switched his attention to Emily, who was introducing herself to him.

"Hello, Mr. Rossi. I'm Emily Dowd, Antonia's friend," I heard her say.

"Dearie me, whatever have you done, Antonia?"

Matron said in a loud whisper as we went into the downstairs loos.

"I...I..." But suddenly everything seemed too much and I felt like crying.

"All right, let's get you sorted out," came Matron's soothing voice as she helped me sit down on the bench that ran along one wall. Nicole sat down beside me and stayed silent as Matron went into one of the toilets and unrolled some loo paper, saying, "This will have to do." Then she let the water run warm and began dabbing away at my hand. Her face took on a disapproving look the more she dabbed. "You really shouldn't have taken the dressing off, Antonia," she said, making a tutting noise with her tongue. "You don't want to get it infected, do you?" She frowned and peered closer. "Hmmm... It looks worse than it is, but I can imagine your dad wouldn't have been too pleased."

"Thank you for..."

Matron's teachery look was gone, thank goodness. "What, for rescuing you?"

I nodded.

"That's all right." Then she chuckled. "I must say I'm quite proud of myself actually. Right, Nicole, I need you to run up to my room for a new dressing. You'll see it on my table."

Nicole was staring anxiously at my plaster. "We'll need something to cover that bloodstain up with, won't we?" Her eyes suddenly sparkled. "*I* know. Nail varnish! I'll raid our cupboards and see what I can find. I'm sure the others won't mind. It's all in a good cause!"

"Right, off you go, dear! You'll need to be quick."

As soon as Nicole had disappeared, Matron said she'd been thinking about attacking the pink blotch with soap and water, because she was concerned that my dad might get anxious about it, but she'd been worried that might make it worse.

"But with the nail varnish it will look as though someone has purposely done me a colourful pattern instead of signing their name," I said. "Won't it?"

I felt so grateful to Matron as she and Nicole and I made our way along to the kitchen. She was reminding me of my grandmother more and more each day, being so gentle and caring, and yet also a bit crazy and very individual. I loved the way she was determined to learn Italian, for example, rather like my grandmother learning to play the accordion. It was lovely to think that I'd be seeing so much more of Nonna after Sunday, but very sad to think that Matron would no longer be in my life.

Emily and my father were just coming out of the kitchen as we approached. The first thing I noticed was that Emily looked relieved to see us. Her eyes flicked from my hand to my plaster and I saw her blink a few times as though she couldn't believe what she was seeing.

"Hi!" I said cheerfully to them both, willing Emily not to say anything about the nail varnish.

"Hello, Toni. All done?" said my dad, glancing at my hand. But like Emily, his eyes went straight to the gleaming blobs of colour on my cast. "Whatever is that?" he asked, with laughter in his voice. "I thought people just wrote messages on casts!"

"No, these days the girls are full of much *brighter* ideas!" said Matron, breaking into her lovely chuckle. "Nail varnish!" she added, rolling her eyes at Papà, as though they were in a grown-ups' conspiracy together. "What will they think of next?"

Papà laughed, then changed the conversation to the Italian evening and said he was sure that the Forest Ash kitchen would be absolutely fine for the cooking and preparing of the food. "I've got some ingredients in the car that I'll leave in the cupboard if that's all right," he went on.

"Of course," said Matron. "I'll be getting on then,

and I'll see you on Saturday, Mr. Rossi."

"And actually I've got to do some gardening now," said Emily.

"Ah," said Papà. "Well, thank you very much for your help, Emily. I'll see you on Saturday!"

"I'll take the ingredients to the kitchen for you, Mr. Rossi," Nicole immediately offered.

I realized that my dad had never met Nicole before. "This is Nicole, my best friend," I said, and Papà shook Nicole's hand and said he was very pleased to meet her. Then we three went outside to the car, and while Nicole hurried back inside with the carrier bag, I stayed with Papà.

"Well you seem to be coping fine, Toni," he said once we were alone.

I nodded and felt my heart yo-yo at the thought of what he would have said if Matron hadn't come to my rescue.

"And your packing is begun?" he went on, his eyebrows raised. I nodded, because I had the feeling he was just about to go, and definitely wouldn't come up to the dorm to check.

He smiled. "Good. Now, Mrs. Pridham says the Italian evening starts about six on Saturday, so Mamma and I will be here at four thirty to give me time to cook."

"Okay." I didn't know what else to say. I think I was still feeling a bit shocked about all that had happened. And it was actually a relief when he went. I waved his car out of sight, then went shakily back inside Forest Ash to find Nicole.

On Friday morning I could hardly concentrate at all during double English, because I was going over and over in my mind the words that my friends and I had worked out together in the dorm the night before. The words that I was about to say to Mrs. Stockton in just a few minutes when the bell went for the end of English.

After lights out we'd all sat up and talked by the light of the little lamps built into the cabin bed headboards. It was such a sad time for all of us, and Nicole and I had been close to tears at the thought that there were only two more nights to go and then Emerald dorm would never be the same again. Then Sasha had got upset too and it had gradually spread round us all.

"We've got to find a way to stop it happening!" Emily had declared dramatically, and that was when Nicole and I had told the others our plan to ask Mrs. Stockton if she'd have a word with Papà to try and convince him that he'd be harming my future career if he took me away from Silver Spires.

But now I was actually here in English class, I found that my heart was beating much faster than usual and my mind was running over and over what I was about to say.

When the bell went, I knew that all my friends who were in set one and set two for English would be crossing their fingers for me and Nicole would be – what did she call it? – yes, sending me her best vibes. And I also knew that when I'd finished talking to Mrs. Stockton I'd find them all waiting outside this room for me.

Around me, everyone was packing away their books or shutting down their computer programs. I was going through those motions too, only very slowly to let the English room empty of students. Mrs. Stockton had dismissed us and now she was tapping away on her laptop at the front.

I carefully eased my way on my crutches to the front of the class. "Er, sorry to disturb you, Mrs. Stockton, but I was worrying if I could have a word with you."

"You were *worrying*?" she said, looking up at me with a smile.

"Wondering," I quickly corrected myself. But

actually "worrying" probably explained it better.

Mrs. Stockton got a chair for me and gave me her full attention. "Yes, Antonia. What can I do for you?"

"It's a bit complicated. You know I'm leaving..."

"Yes, I do. I shall be very sorry to lose you. Your English has come on in leaps and bounds, and you're also a joy to teach. I think all the teachers are feeling sorry..."

"Well, you see, my dad is worried in case something else happens like my accident, because he feels very far away. And I've tried to explain to him that the school can look after me fine, only he won't listen. But there's another important reason why I want to stay at Silver Spires and that's because I want to get better and better at languages...especially English...so I can be an interpreter or a translator when I grow up. But when I try to explain that to Papà he still won't listen, because he's made his mind up about taking me away. So, I wondered if you might be able to talk to him and tell him I'm doing... all right with my English...because you understand about languages...and he might listen to you."

There. I'd managed to get through the whole speech almost word for word as we'd planned it. Now I just had to wait.

Mrs. Stockton's expression was impossible to read. She'd been looking me right in the eyes all the time I'd been talking and now she was still looking at me, as though she was trying to get inside my brain.

"Well obviously I think you're doing brilliantly with your English," she said eventually. "You're excelling." She blinked a few times, as though she'd just been in a daydream and now she was collecting her thoughts. Then she leaned forwards, her hands clasped together, her thumbs rubbing each other. And when she spoke, her voice seemed slower and softer. "Now, this is quite a difficult situation, Antonia, because, as your parents' decision to take you away was very sudden and unexpected, it doesn't really leave us any time to be putting forward an argument against your leaving Silver Spires, however reasonable that argument might seem. Have you... actually talked to your father about wanting to work with languages when you're older?"

"Er...not really."

Mrs. Stockton blinked again and looked down at her clasped hands. "Does that mean not at all?"

I couldn't tell a lie. "Yes."

Mrs. Stockton seemed to be sighing, but not in an impatient way. In a sad, hopeless way. "Would it be fair to say you're clutching at straws because you're so sad about having to leave?" she asked.

My mouth felt suddenly dry as I repeated that phrase, *clutching at straws*, silently to myself. Yes, I could easily work out what it meant. I tried to swallow but my throat was hurting.

I couldn't answer so I nodded and looked down and then felt Mrs. Stockton's hand holding mine.

"I think you need to start by having a frank conversation with your parents about languages. If you truly think you might want to follow this kind of a career when you finish your education, then of course, you're right, it *is* important to be bi- or tri-lingual, and certainly English is the language you'd need most."

I nodded, wondering when I would possibly be able to have this conversation with Papà, and just as though Mrs. Stockton had read my mind, she asked me when I was next seeing my dad.

"Er, he's coming to the Forest Ash Italian evening tomorrow. He's doing the cooking."

"Well, I think the sooner you talk to him, the better. But I hope you understand I'm stepping out of my role as your teacher here, Antonia, and just giving you the kind of advice that I think anyone would give you."

"Yes, I understand…" I said quietly, as I wondered to myself whether or not I might be able to see Papà after school today instead of waiting till he came to do the cooking. Then something else jumped into my mind. "Would you be able to come to our Italian evening, Mrs. Stockton?" I asked impulsively. "I mean, then you might be able to speak to my dad, if I've already talked to him a bit about languages and wanting to be an interpreter and everything?"

Mrs. Stockton leaned back in her chair and gave me a sorrowful look. "I'm sorry, Antonia, but I'm away this weekend. I've got a christening…"

My throat felt even tighter then, because my last hope had just died. "Well, thank you anyway," I managed to mumble as I got up.

"Here…let me…" Mrs. Stockton's chair made a loud scraping noise then toppled backwards, because she'd got up so quickly to get me my crutches. "I'm sorry I haven't been much help."

"It's okay, I'll talk to Papà about languages and… everything."

"Yes, do that. It's a good point. I hope he gives it…consideration."

I was at the door by then. "Thank you," I said again.

Mrs. Stockton smiled, but still with the sorrowful

look on her face so it wasn't really a proper smile, and patted me on the back. "All the best, Antonia."

And I realized as I went outside to join the others that this was her way of saying goodbye.

So then those tears that I'd been holding back filled my eyes and started to roll down my cheeks.

Chapter Nine

"**E**eet ees a – *come si dice, cara? Si,* eet ees a transformation!"

Mamma was using her English and it was so funny to hear it when I'd only ever heard her talking in Italian before. She was in the chair by my bed in Emerald dorm, admiring Emily's hair. Nicole and I were actually sitting on my bed, all dressed up and ready for the evening to start, and the others were still rushing around doing their hair and adding the final touches to their outfits.

All my packing, except for last-minute things, was done. Mamma had done most of it, because I couldn't do it very well with one leg and one hand out of action. My friends had stood round watching in a trembling silence, passing things occasionally, but mainly just staring. At one point I saw Sasha put her arm round Nicole and I deliberately didn't look, but I think Nicole was crying a bit. I think that packing was truly the most horrible task of my life, and I knew I'd never ever forget it.

I'd been helping Papà in the kitchen earlier, slowly and carefully chopping up vegetables, grating cheese and whisking eggs, but I hadn't enjoyed it one little bit, partly because of my hand, but mainly because of my sadness again. I just couldn't shake it off. In fact, it seemed to be deepening. Mamma had taken a walk around the grounds while Papà cooked, because it was quite a hot day and she said she wanted to be outside to feel the English sun on her face. Nicole and the others had all gone to decorate the common room and had given me strict instructions to keep out.

And now we were back together in the dorm, admiring Emily's straight hair. She never usually does anything with her hair except tie it back into a ponytail, which gradually comes loose during the day as most of the hair falls out of the hairband. Matron even has to remind her to brush it sometimes. But tonight she'd done something that we'd persuaded her to do once before for the getting-to-know-you party we had in the first term. She'd borrowed my straighteners and made her hair look lovely and sleek.

"Emily, you look bee-you-tee-fool!" said Mamma, which made us all laugh.

"Thank you, Mrs. Rossi...I mean *Signora* Rossi!" Emily replied.

"No, no, you call me Annalisa, plees."

I was happy because all my friends seemed to really like Mamma, and I also felt proud of her because she looked lovely, dressed up in a flared red and black skirt and a plain black top with red and gold jewellery. She's what my dad calls "petite", and her hair is a big mass of very dark curls just like mine, although mine is a bit longer.

"Eet ees a spetchal evening from Italy so I 'ave bring for you all a geeft from Italy."

"Oh, Mamma, that's brilliant."

"Thank you, Annalisa," chorused my friends.

"Thees are theengs I 'ave weeth me by good fortoon."

"I think Mamma means she just happened to have them with her, because obviously she didn't know about the Italian evening when she and Papà first came over."

Mamma was frowning at me as I spoke and I could tell she was concentrating hard to try and understand what I was saying.

She nodded. "Yes, eet ees correct!"

That made everyone laugh again. But then Mamma was taking things out of a bag. "*Allora*, for Sasha, for zee eyes!"

"Oh thank you, Annalisa," said Sasha, taking the eyeshadow that Mamma was holding out to her. "It's all sparkly. I love it!"

"Thees ees not for old lady. Better for yong girl, I theenk."

"You're not old!" said Sasha and Izzy together.

"So, for Eezzee..." Mamma did a mime of painting her nails as she held out some deep pink nail varnish.

"Oh, that's so cool!" said Izzy. "Thank you very much, Annalisa!"

"Cool! Very cool!" repeated Mamma, as though she was trying out a new word to see if she liked the sound of it. "And for you, Brryonee, and also for Emilee, I theenk...*calzini*!" She turned to me. "What ees...?"

"Oh, they're socks!" said Bryony. "They're brill! Thank you very much!"

"They're totally fab!" said Emily. "Let's swap one,

so we both get to wear both patterns, Bry." Then she turned to me. "Tell your mum she's really clever knowing that Bryony and I are the tomboys."

I quickly translated for Mamma and she said, "Antonia tells a peecture of her friends so I can understand you better."

Mamma sounded so sweet talking in her broken English and I started to wonder whether I'd come across like that when I'd first arrived at Silver Spires. I didn't think so though, because I knew more English than Mamma, even back in September.

"For Neecole and Toni I geev thees – one for each." Mamma was taking off the two little identical silver rings that she nearly always wears on the little finger of her right hand.

Nicole looked anxious. She was shaking her head. "*Non posso...*" she started to say. I'd taught her the Italian for "I can't" only the other day. It comes into our play. "Tell your mum I can't take something that she actually wears!" said Nicole. But I didn't translate, because Mamma was reaching for Nicole's hand. "*Si, si, si, cara!*" She slid one of the rings onto Nicole's little finger and the other one onto mine. "*Perfetto!* Weeth verrry small fingers!"

"Are you sure, Mamma?" I asked her in Italian.

"*Si, si*, yes, yes!" said Mamma, laughing as though

she was still delighted with herself for speaking her bits of English.

"*Molto gentile, grazie,*" said Nicole, smiling at my mum.

Mum's eyes widened as she turned to me and said in Italian, "Nicole speaks Italian very well and with hardly a trace of an accent! What a clever girl!"

I translated for Nicole and she asked me to tell my mum that I was a very good teacher, which made me and Mamma laugh.

"So, I finding Papà for to help heem," said Mamma, getting up to go off to the kitchen where my dad had been cooking away for ages.

"Nearly time!" squeaked Emily excitedly as Mamma went out.

"Your mum's so kind!" said Sasha, coming right up to me and closing her eyes to show me her sparkling eyelids. "Look! Does it suit me?"

"It looks great."

Then Nicole and I put our hands together and compared rings.

"It's such a lovely present." Nicole sighed, tipping her head towards mine.

I nodded, feeling suddenly shaky again at the thought of Nicole and I both wearing our rings.

Would we always wear them? Even in five years' time?

Izzy fluttered her nails. "Nearly dry! It's definitely the coolest nail varnish I've ever worn!"

Then Emily grabbed Bryony's hands and started dancing her around the dorm, doing the occasional high kick to show off Mamma's socks, and saying that they'd got the best present of all.

"Right, make sure we've got everything," I interrupted, wanting to get organized. "I think I'll take a copy of the play script just in case..."

"Shall we go and help your dad take stuff over to the common room?" asked Izzy.

"Yes, then come back for our masks," suggested Bryony.

So that was what we did.

When I awkwardly got myself through the common room door with my crutches, I got a shock. It wasn't yet six o'clock, so there was only Mrs. Pridham and Miss Stevenson in the room, looking very glamorous in floaty dresses and high heels.

"Look!" said Miss Stevenson, straight away. "Your dad bought these!"

She was pointing out the bright pink and soft red

linen tablecloths that covered the trestle tables, and they certainly looked fab.

"Your father has very kindly made a present to Forest Ash of the tablecloths," said Mrs. Pridham. "We're very lucky!"

I was staring at all the sparkling silver table dust, and thinking how perfect it looked.

"That was Nicole's idea!" said Emily. "But don't look at that. Look at the balloons. Red, white and green! Italy's colours. Thanks to yours truly!"

"They're great!" I said. "You've gone to so much trouble."

"And the others did the streamers!" added Emily.

"And the candles," added Izzy.

"It's all wonderful!" I said. "Really, I love it."

"Miss Stevenson and I will collect the rest of the food," said Mrs. Pridham. "Ah, is that the music?"

I handed her a CD.

"Right. Why don't you go and get your masks, all of you, and come down when you hear the music."

"It's going to be nice and loud then!" said Emily.

"Certainly is!" said Miss Stevenson.

When the music started playing it was like a fairy tale. Everyone tumbled out of their dorms, and the

Forest Ash corridors and stairs were suddenly filled with laughter and chattering. We were all in our party clothes, but, better than that, we were all in our masks, so we didn't know who we were talking to as we mingled together and commented on each other's masks and drifted into the common room – well, *I* didn't really drift, I just hobbled in, as usual.

As soon as the track finished, Mrs. Pridham stood on a chair and asked everyone to be quiet for just one moment. "First I want to introduce you to our wonderful chef for the evening, who has produced all this scrumptious authentic Italian food that you see before you, and much more to come out later! May I present...Antonia's father, Signor Rossi!" she said, her voice getting louder in grand announcer's style.

We all clapped and cheered and Papà bowed like a famous film star. Then one of the Year Elevens said that she'd seen him on telly, and asked if she could have his autograph, so then everyone wanted his autograph.

"Hold on, hold on!" said Mrs. Pridham. "All in good time. Now, this is Antonia's mother, Signora Rossi!"

"Annalisa, plees!" called out Mamma, which made everyone smile and cheer even louder than they had for Papà.

"Now," went on Mrs. Pridham, "we're going to be tucking in shortly, but first I have a short film to show you. Can we have the blinds down, please? This is called *Flavours of Italy* and I think you're going to enjoy it."

Most people perched their masks on their heads as they sat down in the various chairs and beanbags and sofas, or just on the floor. The film started with fast, exciting accordion music, the kind we hear at every party we ever go to in Italy, which made me feel like I was back home. On the screen came scene after scene of gondolas in Venice, then shots of everyone dressed up for the spring carnival and close-ups of magnificent masks. After that the film moved to the old bridge in Florence, the vineyards of Tuscany, the fountains in Rome, and the beautiful theatre called La Scala in Milan. And then finally there were loads of wonderful fashion shots. The models strutted up and down the catwalks wearing all kinds of outfit, and I could tell that this was everyone's favourite part of the film, because when the credits rolled at the end there were sighs of disappointment.

I felt a bit nervous then, because it would be our play next and it might seem rather boring and schooly after the film we'd just seen. Someone had pulled the blinds back up and I sensed lots of eyes on me, and wondered if people were feeling sorry for me. Mrs. Pridham had told me that she'd explained to the other students at Forest Ash that I was going back to live in Italy.

"Now I'm going to hand over to Antonia for the next item," she said, smiling at me and stretching out her hands to start off the clapping.

"Ooh, that's me then!" said Matron, moving forwards.

Nicole helped me to hop into my place in the upright chair at the small table, and when the clapping stopped I started miming typing, my heart beating like mad because I just wanted this play to be over with now.

As soon as Nicole started speaking Italian, big cheers went up and she had to wait till they'd died down before she could say her next bit. Then the same thing happened with Matron. But when I started to speak I noticed everyone listened intently, only not in the same way that they listened to the other two. I heard a Year Ten girl whisper to her friend that she'd love to be able to speak completely fluently in another language.

The play was all about a girl who worked in a hotel and was really good at her job, but couldn't help getting cross with a customer who was rude to her, and for that she got the sack from the boss. It was only five minutes long, because it would have been impossible for Nicole and Matron to learn any more, plus no one really understood what was going on in Italian and we didn't want people to be bored. But it was a lovely surprise when we'd finished to hear lots of applause, and one of the Year Nines told us exactly what she thought had been happening in the play, and it was all perfectly right. We each took a special bow and when it was my turn, Matron held me up on one side with Nicole on the other, which raised a laugh.

"Well," said Mrs. Pridham as the clapping died down. "I knew that there was going to be an Italian play this evening, but I must say I had no idea that our very own Forest Ash Matron and one of our Year Seven students would be able to speak Italian to such a high standard after only two terms of spending time with Antonia."

"Antonia gives us confidence, that's why we can do it," said Matron.

There was a little wave of clapping then and someone called out, "Go, Antonia!" It was a Year Ten girl, but I didn't know who she was because she'd still got her mask on. She was standing near

Mamma and Papà, though, and when I glanced in their direction, they both gave me proud looks.

After that it was time for the food. Papà had really worked hard to make six different pizza toppings, all cooked with fresh ingredients. He'd made various other delicious dishes too and there was a buzz in the common room that I don't think there'd ever been before. I noticed Emily spent ages talking to my dad and I knew she'd be talking about the food, because she's really into nutrition from living such a green life with her parents on their farm in Ireland. My dad looked genuinely interested in whatever she was saying. I felt a bit sorry for Mamma, because apart from the film, the only part of the evening that she'd really understood so far was our play.

Mrs. Pridham was standing on the chair again, clapping her hands for attention. "Now, before we all get too full up with this gorgeous Italian meal, I think we should have the special song and dance that Antonia has taught us all."

"*Si, 'Cincirinella'!*" called out Mamma, which made everyone laugh.

"Clear a space! Clear a space!" said Matron. And there was instant activity, with people pushing the sofas and beanbags and things to the sides of the room. Then two Year Ten girls gave me a big surprise by producing a keyboard that was hidden behind a sofa, and one of them started playing the tune to the song.

"I managed to work it out on the piano," she said, smiling at me, "because I thought it might go with more of a swing if we had an accompaniment!"

"*Brava!*" said Mamma as the girl started to play, but Papà didn't look as jolly as Mamma. Maybe he was thinking about how he and I used to sing it together on bike rides, and that made him remember my terrible accident.

I felt a sudden pang of disappointment that I wouldn't be able to dance properly because of my leg. But Nicole dramatically put her hands up to stop the music. "Wait a minute, everyone!" she said. "Izzy and I have to get something from the corridor."

Everyone stood like statues, wondering what ever was going on, then burst into applause as Nicole and Izzy came back in carrying something incredible, which looked like a regular wooden armchair with two long poles attached by rope to the sides, sticking out of the front and back to make four handles. "This is the queen seat we've been making for you, Antonia," said Nicole.

They made their way towards me and I felt like bursting into tears when I saw all the trouble they'd gone to for me. The chair had been painted all over in green, red and white, like the Italian flag, and on each of the slats of the back of the chair was a silver spire made with hundreds and hundreds of sparkling sequins.

"Isn't this just the best?" said Emily, grinning like mad. "Aren't we geniuses?"

"Mr. Cary helped us," Nicole pointed out.

"But we did all the decorating on our own," said Sasha.

"You did the spires! They're amazing!" I breathed.

"And the painting," added Bryony.

"Trouble is, it's a bit awkward to go on the train, I expect," said Emily.

My eyes filled with tears then, but I blinked them away quickly, because Nicole was helping me to sit down on my special throne as the other four held the poles. Then the Year Ten girl started to play again and the "Cincirinella" song and dance began. From my special queen seat I managed to do all the arm actions, which turned out to be brilliant fun after all. At one point I waved across at Papà – a neat little wave as though I was Queen Elizabeth in her state carriage. Papà was standing completely still on his own by a table. He had a small smile on his face, but it was strange because even though he seemed to be looking straight at me, he didn't wave, and it was just as though he was in a bit of a daydream, deep in his own thoughts while the music pounded around him. A few seconds later I noticed that he left the room and realized that, of course, he was thinking about his desserts and was probably going to start bringing them through.

"Just before we move on to puds, we have another little surprise for Antonia," announced Mrs. Pridham when the song had ended. "I think we're all exhausted after so much singing and dancing, so perhaps this would be a good time to sit back and enjoy another film. I'll hand over to Nicole."

That gave me a bit of a shock. Nicole hadn't said a single thing about any other surprises and I couldn't think what the film might be. She squeezed my hand and then went and stood on the chair to make her announcement as Papà slipped back into the room. I thought how anxious she looked.

"Well it's not actually a film, it's a kind of slide show," she said hesitantly. "And it should be Bryony standing here really, because she's the one who's taken most of the pictures, as she's the official Emerald photographer..." There was a ripple of laughter at that. "But anyway, Bryony doesn't like making announcements, so it's me." Nicole looked straight at me then. "It's just a few...memories of our time since we've been at Silver Spires. And we thought you might like to keep the CD as a... souvenir...for when..." Her voice faded out and the room suddenly seemed very still and silent, apart from my heart, which was thumping away for some reason. "Anyway, here it is." She jumped down from the chair as though it would break if she stood there even a second longer, then she sat down at the front and I felt very far away from her. But in a flash Sasha was standing close to me and the slide show began.

I don't know how I managed the next few minutes without crying. It was just a selection of random moments and I know it sounds funny but it almost hurt to watch, and I thought it would have been even worse if Nicole had been right beside me. I guessed she'd thought that too and that was why she'd sat at the front.

I looked at Papà watching the film, still with that half smile on his face, and I really hated him at that moment for what he was doing to break me away from my friends.

There were shots of Emerald dorm and the dining hall, me standing on one leg and waving one of my crutches in the air, Emily staring at the soil in her precious garden, when she'd proudly told us all that her potatoes were growing away under the soil, and then the shot that Bryony had taken straight afterwards of the rest of us all laughing our heads off at the sight of Emily. Then there was Izzy standing in a ballet position holding onto the banister, and Nicole weighed down with both of our bags on her shoulder, and next the whole screen filled with our bright, gleaming masks. Then it was the picture Miss Stevenson took of us all practising "Cincirinella" in the lay-by on our bike ride. Emily looked so funny with her helmet on and it was a relief when someone giggled and Emily piped up, "What?" which made lots more people laugh.

Nicole had been so right when she'd said that it would be a souvenir for me, but as the rest of the shots appeared on the screen I began to wonder whether I'd ever have the courage to watch it back home in Italy, or whether it would just make me feel too far away to bear.

And how could I take the lovely chair back with me, even if it did fit on the train? Those silver spires would always make me homesick for this school that I love so much. I could feel my throat hurting, and when Mrs. Pridham started talking brightly about how we should all get tucking into the delicious puddings now, I knew I wouldn't be able to eat another thing. I was just too sad. I never could have imagined, as Nicole and I had schemed and planned to get these last few days together, that they would finish like this. Mamma had said it would be a lovely end to my time here, but it wasn't.

It was the saddest end there could be.

Chapter Ten

All around me people started drifting towards the pudding table, but there was no excitement left in the room any more. Maybe it was my fault. Maybe I'd let my sadness show too much and now it was seeping out all over Forest Ash, making people move more slowly and speak more quietly.

In one corner of the room I could see Papà leaning forward, talking intently to Mamma, and she was nodding at whatever he was saying. I'd seen that look on his face once before when Nonna had been ill and we'd all worried in case it was more serious than the doctor was telling us.

And now Papà was striding over to Mrs. Pridham as though something had happened – something important that he must tell her about immediately. She nodded too, just like Mamma, lots of little nods, then she clapped her hands and called out loudly: "Sorry, girls, just before we tuck in, Mr. Rossi would like to say something."

The air in our common room felt very still and hot to me. I was wondering what Papà was going to say, but guessed it would be a thank you to everyone for inviting him and Mamma for the evening.

"Forest Ashers," he began, "Annalisa and I would like to thank you all for allowing us to come and share this wonderful evening with you. We have both felt a special magic here in this room and have been trying to work out what it is. Is it the food?" Everyone laughed when Papà said that, but he raised his hand as though he wanted to carry on without any interruptions. "No, it's definitely not the food. The food is good, though I say it myself, but it's not magic." He paused. "So what is it? Is it the music? The masks? The singing? The dancing? The slide show? The film? The play? No, it's none of these things. It's something that's been quietly hovering in this room all evening and I believe it hovers everywhere in Forest Ash…"

Papà sounded truly moved. I looked around subtly and saw that the room was completely still again, everyone hanging on to each word that Papà spoke.

"The magic," he said slowly, "is Forest Ash itself, and what you have all made it." He paused but only for a second. "Or maybe it's Silver Spires itself, I don't know. And that's the trouble. Annalisa and I really didn't know just what a special place this school is. It seems you have to be here to feel it, but we've certainly felt it tonight. And when we look at this wonderful creation that Antonia's close friends have made especially for her, the magic feels so strong that I can't compete with it. So we want to thank you from the bottom of our hearts for this wonderful evening!"

It felt like Papà had finished, but there wasn't much clapping and I understood exactly why. It somehow didn't feel right to burst into applause after that speech. Mrs. Pridham seemed to be taking the lead. She thanked Papà very much and told everyone to enjoy the gorgeous puddings, then she put the music back on and I watched as everyone's stillness unfolded and the room slowly filled up with excitement again.

But I didn't move at all, except to watch as

Papà and Mamma came towards me, and to notice out of the corner of my eye that across the room from me, Nicole was standing like a statue, watching Papà too.

And when he was right up to me I saw that he had tears in his eyes.

"Antonia, we didn't listen to you properly in the hospital when you told us so strongly why you didn't want to leave Silver Spires. No – that's not quite true. We *did* listen, we just didn't understand. Your mother understood as soon as she went to spend time with you and your friends in the dorm while I was cooking. She came to tell me about the magic, but it's no good hearing about it, you have to feel it. And now I've felt it too, I've changed my mind."

My heart was pounding, hurting my ribs with its urgent beating question – what does he mean? What does he mean?

I listened carefully as Papà's voice grew weaker. "Simple as that...I've changed my mind. Of course you must stay at Silver Spires, Antonia. How can we take you away from..." He raised his arm and let it travel round the room, then dropped it at his side as though he was exhausted. "...all this...?"

And then I knew the answer to the question. And

my whole body filled up with the biggest joy I think I've ever felt.

"So she's staying, is she?" came Nicole's thin voice, scraping the silence. I hadn't even noticed her joining us.

"Yes," said Papà, his eyes flicking from me to Nicole and back to me.

My heart stopped pounding so painfully and a wonderful joy took its place as Nicole shouted out above the music. "She doesn't have to leave after all! She's staying at Silver Spires! Antonia's staying!"

And like an answering cry in the wild, Emily's voice came back loud and clear: "Go, Antonia! No, I mean, *stay*, Antonia!"

Then laughter erupted in every corner of the room, followed by big cheering, even from the much older girls who don't really know me. My friends were jumping up and down and thanking Papà, as though he'd saved my life. I was so happy I wanted to cry, but I couldn't because Nicole was hugging me tight.

"You're not going after all! Oh, Antonia, isn't it amazing?"

Then we were all hugging each other and eventually I came to Mamma and she squeezed me so tight I thought I'd burst. "*Mia cara*," she said softly into my hair. "*Felice adesso?* 'Appy now?"

I'd started to cry by then for some unknown reason, so I couldn't answer. I just nodded into her hair.

Papà had moved away and was talking to Mrs. Pridham when I looked up, but his eyes met mine and I mouthed "Thank you" to him. All he did was put a hand up as though I was thanking him for a piece of pizza and it was nothing. But I know my dad and I knew he was too emotional to talk to me at that moment. And I also knew there'd be plenty of time to talk later – before they flew home and then all through the holidays in three weeks' time. But now wasn't the time for talking. It was the time for celebrating.

And it was lovely Matron who turned the music up loudly and flung the window open dramatically. "Let the whole of Silver Spires hear our happiness!" she shouted above the noise.

Nicole gave me a tight hug then with her cheek right next to mine and out of the corner of my eye I was aware of a little flash and I thought, *That's going to be a great photo. Another lovely memory.*

But then I remembered I didn't need the memory any more. I could just live for the moment. So I leaned on Nicole and hopped my way over to the pudding table, and as everyone patted me on the

back and told me they were so happy, I felt that
wonderful warm magic that Papà had talked about.

I really felt it.

Want to know more about the
Silver Spires girls?

Or try a quiz to discover which
School Friend you're most like?

You can even send Silver Spires e-cards
to your best friends and post your own
book reviews online!

It's all at

www.silverspiresschool.co.uk

Check it out now!

Antonia's Favourite Recipes

Our Silver Spires Italian evening meant the world to me, and Papà's home-made food made it extra-special. Now you can try our yummy pizza toppings too!

★ Traditional Neopolitan Pizza

Ingredients:
3 tablespoons olive oil
1 clove garlic (finely chopped or crushed)
1 tin chopped tomatoes
Salt and freshly ground black pepper
2 teaspoons oregano
4 tablespoons olive oil
Ready-made pizza base

What to do:
1. Preheat the oven to 220°C.
2. Carefully heat the oil in a saucepan, then add the crushed garlic and fry gently for just a few seconds.
3. Add the tin of chopped tomatoes.
4. Season with the salt and pepper, then cover and simmer for 15-20 minutes.
5. Place your pizza base on a baking tray.

6. Spoon out the tomato mix over the pizza base, as close to the edges as you can.

7. Sprinkle with the oregano and drizzle with the remaining oil.

8. Bake in the oven for 10-15 minutes, then serve hot – yum!

To turn this basic Neopolitan pizza into something even more tasty, just add the ingredients below between steps 6 and 7.

★ For **Pizza Margherita**, add shredded mozzarella and 3-4 fresh basil leaves.

★ For **Pizza Prosciutto e Funghi**, add finely sliced mushrooms, ham and shredded mozzarella.

★ For **Pizza Quattro Stagioni** (Four Seasons), add shredded mozzarella, and then arrange tinned quartered artichoke hearts, black olives, finely sliced mushrooms and finely sliced ham (one ingredient to each quarter of the pizza).

★ For **Pizza ai Quattro Formaggi** (Four Cheese), we traditionally add shredded pecorino, gorgonzola, groviera (Swiss Cheese) and fontina cheeses on top of the usual mozzarella. But why not try it with whatever your favourite cheeses are?

Buon appetito! *Antonia*

Now read on for a sneak preview of

Success at Silver Spires

"Can you help with my stupid hair, Sasha?" said Emily, sighing dramatically.

I was the only one ready, so I jumped up from the bench in the changing rooms where we were sitting, and took the hairband she was holding out to me. It was going to be quite a challenge getting Emily's thick wavy hair squeezed into the small, thin band. No wonder she was having problems.

My best friend, Izzy, pulled a scrunchie out of her pocket. "Try this, Sash." And when I'd just about managed to make a fairly neat but rather stubby ponytail for Emily, Mrs. Truman, the PE teacher, clapped her hands, calling us all to attention.

It was the first PE lesson of the summer term and we knew things might be different from the last two terms. There's always so much going on at Silver Spires – it's just the best boarding school ever.

"Okay, girls, let's have a bit of hush and I'll tell you about the sport on offer in the summer."

Bryony and Emily, who are also in my close group of friends, gave each other quick, excited looks, as though they were dying to hear the news, and I thought how great it must be to be able to get excited about something like sport. I'm just not a sporty person, so whatever Mrs. Truman was about to say, it somehow didn't feel like it had anything to do with me...

To find out what happens next, read

Success at Silver Spires

Complete your

School Friends

collection!

About the Author

Ann Bryant's School Days

Who was your favourite teacher?

At primary it was Mr. Perks – we called him Perksy. I was in his class in Year Six, and most days he let me work on a play I was writing! At secondary, my fave teacher was Mrs. Rowe, simply because I loved her subject (French) and she was so young and pretty and slim and chic and it was great seeing what new clothes she'd be wearing.

What were your best and worst lessons?

My brain doesn't process history, geography or science and I hated cookery, so those were my least favourite subjects. But I was good at English, music, French and PE, so I loved those. I also enjoyed art, although I was completely rubbish at it!

What was your school uniform like?

We had to wear a white shirt with a navy blue tie and sweater, and a navy skirt, but there was actually a wide variety of styles allowed – I was a very small person and liked pencil-thin skirts. We all rolled them over and over at the waist!

Did you take part in after-school activities?
Well I loved just hanging out with my friends, but most of all I loved ballet and went to extra classes in Manchester after school.

Did you have any pets while you were at school?
My parents weren't animal lovers so we were only allowed a goldfish! But since I had my two daughters, we've had loads – two cats, two guinea pigs, two rabbits, two hamsters and two goldfish.

What was your most embarrassing moment?
When I was in Year Seven I had to play piano for assembly. It was April Fool's Day and the piano wouldn't work (it turned out that someone had put a book in the back). I couldn't bring myself to stand up and investigate because that would draw attention to me, so I sat there with my hands on the keys wishing to die, until the Deputy Head came and rescued me!

To find out more about Ann Bryant visit her website: www.annbryant.co.uk

For more fun and friendship-packed reads check out www.fiction.usborne.com